THE PHENOM

A Brown and McNeil Novel

by the Author of

The Murder Gambit

BOOKS BY FRANK LAZARUS

The Murder Gambit

The Phenom

Recruiting Murder

April Fool

The Good, The Bad, & The Ugly: 102 First Dates

Is Anything Alright?

COPYRIGHT

DEDICATION

To my grandchildren:

Halle, Felicity,

Noah, Riley, & Jack

Pop-Pop always loves you!

CHARACTER CHEAT SHEET

BOOKMARK THIS PAGE TO REFERENCE THE PRIMARY CHARACTERS

Bo Campbell – The Phenom and accused murderer

Hugh Campbell – Bo's Father

Winnie McNeil Campbell – Bo's mother and daughter of James McNeil

Claudia Campbell – Bo's sister

Kendrick Campbell – Bo's older brother

Jessica Marks – Bo's platonic girlfriend

Carl Watkins – Bo's best friend and teammate

Sherman Claxton – Murder Victim, Bo's friend, West Philly High player

James McNeil – Bo's grandfather and friend of Detective Vernon McNeil

Linda McNeil – James' wife

Rasheed McNeil – James' son and CEO of PhillyBeats

Vernon Brown – Senior Detective and friend of James McNeil

Ronnie Brown – Vernon's Wife

Roberta Rumson – Vernon Brown's partner

David Kasper – Philadelphia District Attorney

Michelle Pugh – Assistant District Attorney

Fred Chasnoff – Bo's Attorney

Melanie Wexler – Chasnoff Associate

Myron Rosen – Overbrook Basketball Coach

Reggie McIntosh – Big Mac, Overbrook Assistant Coach

Brahim Jones (Heem) – Inherited Big Earl's Drug gang

Spooky Little – Heem's was overseer at Overbrook

Spanky Waters – Heem's runner at Overbrook

Damian Mitchell – Heem's overseer at West Philly

Dwight Bridges – Heem's runner at West Philly/Moves later to JRo

Mr. B – Reclusive new Drug Boss

Jason Rogers (JRo) – Mr. B's Front man

Chapter 1

February 12, 2022

Overbrook High School in Philadelphia is legendary, at least with Philadelphians and basketball fans. It is in the western section of the city and has sent over twenty graduates to the NBA including Wilt Chamberlain, Walt Hazzard, Wally Jones, Lewis Lloyd, and Andre McCarter. Students are called The Hilltoppers, *but no one is certain what hill they are on top of.*

The student body is mostly Black and Asian, but that was not always the case. From the 1950s through the 1970s, it included about fifty-percent whites. Like all inter-city schools, crime and violence were not unknown, but today's headlines would not be like any other.

———

At 4:30 Monday afternoon, Detective Vernon Brown, his partner Roberta Rumson, and two Philadelphia PD uniformed patrol officers walked into the gymnasium of Overbrook High School. They knew who they were looking for: number thirteen, Bo Campbell.

Bo Campbell was the most talked about student-athlete in the city; perhaps the country. Even though Chamberlain did not wear number thirteen at Overbrook High, he was best known for wearing that number in college and for three different NBA teams. Campbell wanted everyone to know that Wilt's greatness was what he aspired to.

In his first three years at Overbrook, Bo had lived up to that hype, winning all but two games, and three Public and City Championships. As a senior, Bo was mulling over his scholarship offers.

Vernon Brown was a 55-year-old, 30-year veteran of the Philadelphia Police Department, the last 23 years as a detective. He had worked his entire career out of the 18th District at 55th and Pine

Streets in West Philadelphia. He grew up a mile away from the district headquarters and attended Overbrook's arch-rival West Philadelphia High School. Brown still lived in West Philadelphia.

Brown was 6'2" tall and still lean and mean. He had a crew cut that was now 80% gray. To hide a mole on the right side of his lip, he kept a well-groomed mustache. He was the senior detective in the district. He was assigned the toughest cases, but he knew this might be one he wished away.

His partner, Roberta Rumson, was a 32-year-old Black woman. She was promoted to detective four years ago and was assigned to Brown, whose prior partner, Chuck Jankowski, had been dismissed for helping himself to cocaine during a drug bust.

At the Overbrook gym, Myron Rosen, the head coach, was overseeing a full-court scrimmage. Brown seemed unphased and led his ensemble onto the court toward

Campbell. Rosen saw them at once and whistled a stop to the scrimmage. Brown walked toward Rosen flashing his badge.

"May I help you, officers?" Rosen asked.

"We're good, coach. We are here to make an arrest."

"What the hell do you mean interrupting my practice here? This couldn't wait?" Rosen was furious and stepped in front of Brown.

"Get out of my face, Coach. Justice doesn't revolve around your practice. Step aside and let us do our job."

Brown walked toward Campbell, and said, "Bo Campbell, we are arresting you for the murder of Sherman Claxton. You have the right to remain silent."

"What are you talking about? You know I didn't kill Sherman. Stop, please?" A crying and hysterical Bo Campbell fell to his knees.

Bo had learned about the death of his buddy Sherman Claxton yesterday when this same Detective Brown called his grandfather, James McNeil. When his parents told him, Bo was devastated and spent the day in his room crying. But no one had suggested that

Campbell was involved in Claxton's death. He had been to a Villanova game at The Palestra Saturday night with Sherman, and his friend was fine when they got off at different subway stops on the way home.

Bo had decided to come to school and practice today, but now wished he had not. *How could he have expected this?*

The Unis handcuffed him as Brown read Campbell his Miranda rights, and led him off the court and toward the exit. Staying behind, Brown asked Rosen if they could speak.

Rosen yelled over to his Assistant Coach, Reggie McIntosh, "Mac, can you take over, please? Same stuff, work on the inbound plays."

Easier said than done; the stunned players gawked at Campbell being led out of the gym. They huddled into small groups trying to grasp what had happened; their star player, their leader and friend, was being arrested for murder.

After ten minutes, McIntosh blew the whistle and gathered the kids around him. "OK, guys. I wish I could tell you what's going on but I don't know much more than you do. Saturday night, Sherman Claxton, a friend of Bo's, was shot on 52nd Street. I understand your heads are not in this practice right now, so let's call it a day. Maybe we'll all know more in the morning. I'll talk to Coach about having a counselor available as soon as possible for anyone who might wish to talk to one. OK, dismissed!"

Rosen had led Brown and Rumson to his office. "There must be a mistake, officers. Bo's a good kid and could not have killed anyone."

"No one wishes that were true more than me, Coach, but it is what it is. I can't discuss the details or the evidence, but we will need to interview you and many of the players. I'll call you to schedule that. We can do it here rather than at the station."

"We'll cooperate. Anything we can do to get Bo out of this mess. I hate to be crass here, but the playoffs start in two weeks. Any chance Bo will be available?"

"Not for me to say, but even if he is permitted bail, you want him exposed to the ridicule and harassment this will bring, perhaps even some revenge violence?" Brown replied.

"I guess you're right. Have Bo's parents been contacted?"

"Next on my list! Thanks, Coach. I'll be in touch soon."

Vernon Brown was a good friend of James McNeil, Bo Campbell's grandfather. Brown and McNeil had become friendly three years earlier when Brown was investigating the hit-and-run death of McNeil's father in West Philadelphia. They worked together to find the perpetrator.

When Brown and Rumson returned to his car, he knew he could not procrastinate any longer. He needed to make the call he dreaded.

"Yo, Vern, what's going on, bruh?"

"Things could be better, James. But unfortunately, we just arrested Bo for the murder of Sherman Claxton. I'm very sorry, James."

"You gotta be shitting me. You know Bo, he ain't killed nobody."

"Let's get together. Usual place? Eight in the morning? I'm going over to tell Bo's parents. Want to meet me there?"

"Not a chance, Vern, but I'll see you in the morning. I'm telling you again, you got the wrong man."

Chapter 2

February 12, 2022, 8:15 PM

The Commonwealth of Pennsylvania required a Preliminary Arraignment Hearing within six hours of arrest. In Philadelphia, this would be conducted at Philadelphia's Municipal Court at the Stout Center for Criminal Justice. The new Criminal Justice building was opened in 1994 to alleviate the strain on the city's other court rooms in Philadelphia's City Hall, just two blocks away. In 2012, it was renamed in honor of the late Justice, Juanita Kidd Stout.

The purpose of the Preliminary Arraignment Hearing was twofold; first, the judge would officially read the charges against the defendant, and second, to determine bail, if appropriate. In Pennsylvania, as in almost all other states, those charged with murder were not eligible for bail.

The Campbell family, however, had every intention of pleading for bail, not wanting Bo to spend even one night in jail. The odds were against them. Bo's sister, Claudia, was an attorney, but with no criminal experience. They had no time to find a criminal attorney, but she had cashed in a favor and called a friend of a friend, and had received prepping on what to expect, and how to handle the case.

Sensing this could become a high-profile case, the Philadelphia District Attorney's office sent Assistant District Attorney Michelle Pugh to be present at the hearing.

Bo was brought into the courtroom by the bailiff. His parents had bought him a blue dress shirt, gray slacks, and a sports coat. He was rightfully scared; looking around the room first, and then to his parents, the only other two in the courtroom. Winnie Campbell was sobbing with her handkerchief trying to catch the tears. Her husband, Hugh, tried unsuccessfully to comfort her.

The bailiff exclaimed, "All rise!" and they did. The Honorable Judge Emmett P. Ferguson was summoned to oversee this hearing and seemed anxious to dispense with it and return home. Judge Ferguson was a 63-year-old jurist who had been elected to the bench in 1995 and has been re-elected ever since. He was known to be tough but fair, the best any defendant could hope for.

"Whom do we have here tonight?" he asked.

"Your Honor, I am Claudia Campbell, representing the defendant, Bowman Campbell."

"Thank you, Ms. Campbell, and I see the District Attorney's office represented. What brings you to a Pre-Arraignment, Ms. Pugh?"

"Our office just wanted a presence here tonight, Your Honor."

"Very well, please be seated. Mr. Campbell, please stand. While the arresting officer may have read the charges against you, it is the purpose of this court to read and make certain you understand these charges. Do you understand?"

"Yes, sir."

Judge Ferguson read the murder charges and, in conclusion, stated, "Since bail is not available in a murder case, would there be any other matters for us to discuss this evening?"

Claudia stood and said, "Your Honor, despite the guidelines calling for no bail in a murder case, exceptions are permitted at the discretion of the Court and we believe there are extenuating circumstances. My client's innocence aside, the defendant is an eighteen-year-old high school student expecting to graduate in June. He lives at home with his parents and has no criminal or juvenile record. He has a number of full scholarship offers to attend college in September. His incarceration would put his future in severe jeopardy, and the District Attorney's office has not offered a motive or even that this is a first-degree murder case. Therefore, we humbly ask the Court for bail consideration under the special exception considerations allowed by Pennsylvania law."

"Nice speech, Counselor. Care to comment, Ms. Pugh?" Judge Ferguson turned to the ADA.

Michelle Pugh stood slowly, gathering her thoughts. This would be the first test to measure the Judge's attitude about the case, and she wanted him as an advocate.

"Your Honor, the People object to bail consideration. Whether we make the charges first, or second degree, no bail is warranted under either. Nor do we see that special circumstances exist for the court to make an exception to the no-bail guidelines. To do so would be highly unusual, Your Honor."

"Counselor, I am a highly unusual individual, and I will split the baby. I will allow House Arrest for one week with electronic monitoring with two hours a day for exercise and visits with his attorney permitted. I will schedule the Preliminary Hearing one week from today at 10:00 in the morning. At that time, both parties may make their case, and should the defendant be remanded for trial, we will revisit bail. Good evening, everyone."

They all stood, the judge left, and the Campbell family all looked relieved. At least for a week, Bo would continue to be safe at home.

Chapter 3

July 10, 2018

Most big cities had a basketball culture, and Philadelphia was the authority on that culture.

Kids started playing in elementary school, then progressed through middle school, and then for some, high school. But the real action was in the schoolyards, playgrounds, and gymnasiums, where kids would hone their skills and take on the best competition right there in the hood.

Three locations in the Philadelphia area attracted the best players from local high schools, colleges, and the pros. Haddington Recreation Center, and Tustin Playground, both in West Philadelphia, were legendary, and the summer leagues were well-scouted by college and professional scouts. Narberth Playground in suburban Narberth gave players a third option.

Tustin Playground was a block away from Overbrook High School and thus was the home court for Chamberlain, Hazzard, and Jones in the '50s and '60s. Later, Kobe Bryant would come in from the suburbs to cut his teeth there.

A young player who had yet to play his first high school game was the featured attraction tonight at Tustin Playground. Bo Campbell recently graduated from Beeber Middle School and would start at Overbrook High in September. At 6'5" and growing, his potential was unlimited.

Bo was an outlier in today's basketball world; totally unselfish. Some experts feared that he might be too unselfish and that his scoring stats might not attract the scouts only looking at box scores. It would be their loss. Bo was focused on fifteen; his goal was to get fifteen points, rebounds, and assists per game and throw in another five or six block shots. But most importantly, his team needed to WIN! If the game was close, Bo would take over.

Bo was the youngest player in the high school league, but he was confident he would not be overmatched. He knew his teammates. Three were future teammates at The Brook, and the other three were from West Catholic and Bonner High Schools.

Back in the day, as they say, basketball was more straightforward. Teams had two guards, two forwards, and a center. In today's more specialized world, you had a point guard, a shooting guard, a power forward, a small forward, and a center. Bo, of course, could and would play them all, depending on the defense, the score, and the player matchups.

Tonight's game went as expected, at least according to Bo's plan. His team had a slight lead through most of the game. Bo scored but focused on setting up his teammates, rebounding, and playing solid defense. Bo was not dominating but held his own. His coach called a time-out with four minutes remaining in the game and Bo's team leading by four points.

Bo's buddy and point guard, Carl Watkins, asked, "What the hell you doing, Bo? Game's too close. A bucket or two from you might help."

"Whatever, bruh!"

When play resumed, the opponent's best player took the ball at the key, with a spin move, went to the foul line, and went up for the shot. Bo anticipated the move, blocked the shot, and scampered for the loose ball. Scooping it up in full stride, he went the length of the court, jammed it with two guys hanging on him, and was fouled. He made the follow-up free throw.

On the next trip down court, the opponents missed, Bo's team rebounded, and slowed the pace. Then with ten seconds remaining on the shot clock, the ball came to Bo, who feinted to drive, then took a step-back jumper for three. IT'S GOOD!

With a ten-point lead, Bo's team coasted to victory. Players shook hands and man hugged. Sweaty and tired, Bo still wanted to seek out number seven, the opposing team's top scorer.

"Yo, bruh, nice game! You made me work way too hard. My name's Bo. Where do you go to school?"

"Going into my sophomore year at West Philly. Name is Sherman Claxton. Nice game yourself."

"I guess we'll be seeing a lot of each other. I start at Overbrook in September."

"For sure, bruh, but I'm sure I'll see you out here before then. You playing out at Narberth too?"

"Of course! See you Thursday? They are assigning teams. Maybe we'll get on the same team!"

"That would be cool. See you then."

Chapter 4

February 13, 2022

The usual place meant the Dunkin' Donuts at 52nd and Chestnut Streets in West Philadelphia.

Vernon Brown had met James McNeil at this very spot three years ago. Then, Brown had been assigned to the hit-and-run murder of McNeil's father, Lincoln. With McNeil's participation, Brown eventually killed the perpetrator, a Russian hitman. In an elaborate financial scheme, Vladimir Petrov had been contracted to kill dozens of senior citizens to collect their life insurance proceeds.

Brown always arrived before James, so he had his coffee and a glazed donut with rainbow jimmies waiting when he arrived. They man-hugged and sat.

"You know, my wife and daughter are totally freaked, and I must admit, so am I. What the fuck, Vern? You know Bo could not have done this." James took a seat across from his friend.

"I understand, James, but there is too much heat on this one. I could not ignore the evidence. My captain asked me if I wanted to recuse myself because of our relationship, but I thought it best to stay involved."

"I appreciate that, Vern. What can you tell me?"

He caught Brown with a mouthful of donut, Vern swallowed, took a sip of coffee, and replied, "You know I shouldn't be discussing evidence with anyone, James, so please keep this between us. They found a gun matching the description of the one used to shoot Sherman and a kilo of heroin in Bo's locker at school. We have a search warrant for the house, and we'll be conducting it tomorrow."

"Shit! You know, evidence could be planted, and obviously was, in this situation. Is there more?"

"Maybe. What can you tell me about Bo's relationship with Sherman Claxton?"

"I think you know, Vern, they met in the summer before Bo started at The Brook. Sherman was at West Philly and a year ahead of him. They got close over that summer and remained friends. I can't imagine why Bo might want to hurt Sherman."

"How did the Pre-Arraignment go last night?"

"His sister Claudia handled that, and it went OK, I guess; Bo is home with a monitor for another week, at least. But Claudia is not a criminal attorney and does not want to represent him after today. Got any suggestions?"

"If you feel you need or want a Black attorney, then Gladys Gresham would be my choice, but if you want the best, I'd go for Fred Chasnoff.

Pausing, brushing crumbs off of the table, and taking the last gulp of his coffee, Brown said, "Look, James, this will be tough on us both, more on you for sure. No matter what, I'm your friend. You need to know that and don't forget it. We'll get through this, brother."

"See you in court, Vern!"

"Yep!"

On his way home, James called his daughter Winnie and asked if he might stop over for dinner and relay his discussion with Vernon Brown; he'd order pizza when he got there. Of course, she agreed.

James arrived at 6:00. Parking on these narrow, one-way streets was always a challenge as many homes had two, sometimes three, cars and few opted to use their garages. He noticed that Claudia was already there; her car added to the crowd. But he found a tight spot six houses down and squeezed into it.

The Campbells lived on the 5600 block of Arlington Street in the Wynnefield section of West Philadelphia. The row homes looked smaller than they were as they were twice as deep as they were wide. The white flight hit this Wynnefield section in the '70s and within five years the neighborhood went from 100% white to 90% Black. But this was a solid, middle-income, working-class neighborhood. The two synagogues were converted to Baptist Churches.

When James walked in, the entire family was waiting. His daughter Winnie had set the dining room table for the six of them. They had not waited to order the pizza, and her husband Hugh had cut them and laid them out on the kitchen table. Claudia was putting the finishing touches on a salad. Bo and his brother Kendrick were watching *SportsCenter* on ESPN.

James asked, "Did we really need that third pizza, Hugh?"

"Have you seen Kendrick and Bo eat lately, James? Two are for them. The third is for us four. Can I grab you a beer, James?"

"Sure, whatever you got."

James was a frequent visitor, so formalities were unnecessary. But Winnie rejected the suggested paper plates. They loaded their plates in the kitchen and took their usual seats in the dining room.

Despite the elephant in the room, they engaged in the usual small talk but sooner or later, the elephant needed to be heard.

James repeated what Brown had told him, and said, "Our first decision, I guess, is an attorney. Claudia, what do you think?"

Bo quickly exclaimed, "I want Claudia to be my lawyer."

Claudia turned to her brother. "Bo, you know criminal law is not my specialty. If it makes sense, I'd be glad to sit second chair, but we need the best we can find or afford."

James added, "Fred Chasnoff was suggested to me, and I had a preliminary discussion with him. He said he could be available and work with us on his fee. He had received a call from Coach Rosen, and, as an Overbrook alum, Chasnoff knew of Bo."

"Wow, Chasnoff is the best and would be great," Claudia offered.

"Can we agree to let Claudia work with Chasnoff? I do not think having five of us contacting the guy would be appropriate." James stared at Bo's father, Hugh.

Hugh Campbell stared back. "What's with this Detective buddy of yours, James? Is he for or against us?"

"He's a detective, Hugh. He is for us, but he's in a tough situation. And the DA's office calls the shots, so not much Vernon can do except chase the evidence."

Bo asked, "What about the playoffs?"

James replied, "I spoke with Coach Rosen, and we agreed it is best for you to sit out. Your presence would be a distraction at best and, at worst, would invite protests, name-calling, and even potential violence."

Bo challenged him, "We lost the beginning of last season because of COVID, and now my senior year, I've got to sit out the end of my high school career?"

James felt for his grandson, but added, "Bo, I know this isn't fair, but we will get to the bottom of this, and that is the most important thing. You know how the coach feels."

Hugh said, "You spoke with Coach Rosen? Maybe I need to talk to him. How will his sitting out affect Bo's scholarship offers?"

"You are welcome to discuss with the Coach, Hugh, if you feel differently, but that will be his decision. And I cannot speak for the scholarships. I would suspect those will await the outcome of the trial. I think our focus right now needs to be on Bo and his defense."

Chapter 5

August 15, 2018

Everyone knew that the Narberth Summer League High School division championship would come down to The Westies and The Southsiders.

Bo, Sherman Claxton, and Carl Watkins were on The Westies. The Southsiders were made up of outstanding veteran players from Southern High, PET Charter, and Saint John Neumann High Schools. In Philly, the Public and Catholic Schools only played against each other for the City Championship, but the Summer Leagues allowed them to see and compete against the city's best.

The Westies and Southsiders played twice this summer, each winning once. The Southsiders' win had an asterisk, as Bo sat out the second half with a stomach bug. Tonight's game had been well publicized all over social media, and the stands were packed. It was being streamed locally, sponsored by TastyKake, a Philadelphia-based snack food company.

The game started quickly and got faster after that. Both teams wanted to run. The shooting was erratic. At halftime, The Westies led 37-33. The Southsiders were paced by 6'2" point guard Kevin Andrews, who would be a senior this year at Southern High. The Westies were playing in a zone, and Andrews was penetrating, then hitting the jumper from the foul line or going all the way to the hoop. His fourteen points were high for the game.

Westies coach, Sonny Hilliard, decided to switch to a man-to-man defense making it more difficult for Andrews to penetrate. Immediately, Bo volunteered to cover Andrews. Coach Hilliard asked, "Are you sure he's not too quick for you, Bo?"

"Nah, I got this, Coach! And he won't shoot threes over me."

"OK, Bo, we'll give it a go, but we still need some offense out of you."

"Yes, sir!"

They discussed the other defensive matchups and some offensive strategies. Then, it was time to play!

The second half did not resemble the first half in any way. Both teams wanted a slower pace to avoid mistakes down the stretch. But it didn't matter. Bo was up to the task of covering Andrews, and with their star bottled up, the Southsiders were frustrated and disorganized. The Westies slowly grew the lead and won the game by a score of 69-59. Bo led all scorers with twenty-two points and held Andrews to six points in the second half.

Coach Hilliard gathered the guys and congratulated them, wished them well in their upcoming high school seasons, and reminded them to make good decisions.

Perhaps, starting tomorrow. A couple of the older guys had planned an After Party at George's Hill, a secluded area in Fairmount Park known for its foggy windows, empty beer bottles, and discarded condoms; oh yeah, and a cool view of the city.

There would be girls and beer. What else was needed?

Chapter 6

February 14, 2022

Claudia Campbell drove her RAV4 into the city with Bo; the five-mile trek from West Philly should take ten minutes but always required thirty. She decided to avoid the Schuylkill Expressway and opted for West River Drive, which ran parallel to the Expressway and the Schuylkill River. She passed Boathouse Row on the other side of the river. Many of the local colleges and rowing clubs kept their shells and equipment in these hundred-year-old boat houses. Several had added elaborate dining and party rooms and rented them out to the public. At night, the boat houses were all lit up and the view was spectacular.

The West River Drive merged into the Benjamin Franklin Parkway at the Art Museum, always famous to art lovers, but since Rocky trained on its steps, well known to all. And at any time of the day or night, there were a dozen tourists lined up taking pictures next to the bronze life-size Rocky statue.

Claudia parked in an underground lot at Liberty Place in the heart of Center City. They had an eleven o'clock appointment with Fred Chasnoff at the offices of Goldfarb, Donahue, and Chasnoff, LLC. On the ride into the city, Bo had a lot of questions for Claudia; she answered the easy ones and deferred the tougher ones to Chasnoff.

Two blocks from City Hall, Liberty Place was best known for being the first building to be taller than the top of William Penn's hat on his statue atop City Hall. That was in 1986 and, once that gentlemen's agreement of local developers had been broken, many new, taller buildings now obscured City Hall from the Philadelphia skyline.

Fred Chasnoff's assistant showed them to the conference room where Chasnoff was awaiting them, sitting next to another woman. He stood, introduced himself, shook hands, and offered politely declined beverages.

Chasnoff had a presence; six foot, two inches, lean, well groomed, dark hair showing some gray at the temples, and dressed impeccably in a dark blue suit, white French cuff shirt, and Vitaliano silk tie.

"I have asked Melanie Wexler to sit in. Mel heads our Criminal Defense Team and she'll be handling much of the investigation and preparation of Bo's defense."

Wexler smiled at Bo and Claudia. Wexler could have stepped out of the pages of *Elle* magazine; 5'10", slim, shoulder-length blond hair, and attired in a slimming royal blue dress, with expense jewelry, save for the Apple Watch worn on her left wrist.

"Has your sister explained the process, Bo?" Chasnoff asked.

"Yeah, I think so," Bo answered nervously while biting his gums and fidgeting in his chair.

"We know some of their evidence, the gun, and heroin, but I suspect they might have more. We will claim that the evidence was planted. What concerns me, Bo, is a motive. They will need one to convince a jury that you had a reason to kill Claxton. Any idea what that might be?"

"I have no idea, Mr. Chasnoff. Sherman and I were good friends. We hung out and played a lot of ball together. I can't imagine why anyone would think I killed him."

"When, where, and how did you two meet?"

"It was the summer of 2018. I had graduated from Beeber Middle School and was playing a lot of summer ball, getting ready for Overbrook in the fall. We met at Tustin, and we were on different teams. After the game, I introduced myself, and we wound up on the same team at Narberth. Even though he was going to West Philly, we lived close enough to hang out and play together. I'd say he has become my second-best friend behind Carl Watkins."

"Do you have any enemies, Bo? Have you gotten into any squabbles or fights, either on the court, over girls, or anyone at all?"

"I'm a competitive guy and do my share of trash-talking. That has led to a couple of pushing and shoving scraps, but nothing serious. Some guys may be jealous of the attention I get, but not much I can do about that. I think I'm tight with all my teammates. No fights over girls."

"Either of you have girlfriends?"

"No, but I hang with Jessica Marks a lot, but Sherm didn't have a girl."

"Jessica a white girl?"

"How'd you guess? Yeah, she's the sister of Neil Marks. I played with Neil in the Narberth league a few years ago, and Jessica came with him to most of the games. She's my age. Neil is two years older and plays college ball at Lafayette. Jessica and I are tight, but no serious romantic thing going on."

"And where does Jessica go to school?"

"Lower Merion."

"Talk to me about the drug culture in school and the Hood."

"I'm probably not the best guy to answer that. You gotta know I'm not into anything, never even smoked a joint; won't try any of it. But sure, there's plenty of weed around. A couple of guys on the team used it. I also see some Oxy and China Girl around. But meth, H, and whatever, I know nothing. You need to understand the dynamics of school. You got the athletes, the students or nerds, and gangstas. Of course, there is some crossover; I'd like to think of myself as a student-athlete, but for the most part, these groups hang together."

"And how about Claxton?" Claudia asked.

"Sherm was a freshman at Widener, a D3 school. He got an academic scholarship there. He is definitely a ballplayer, but I do know he experimented with Oxy. Asked me a couple of times to try it, but I told him no way. I know he was not hooked on it, and I told him not to use it in my company. He respected that."

Chasnoff said, "Someone killed him, Bo, and framed you. So first, did he have any known enemies, owe someone for Oxy, any girls figure into the story, or just anything at all that would help us point the jury in another direction? This is complicated, Bo. Not only did someone want Claxton dead, but they also wanted you to be blamed. There needs to be something connecting this."

"I think about that all the time, sir, but as yet, I can't figure it out, shaking his head in wonderment.

"You have any further questions, Claudia?"

"Not really, Fred. Is there anything we should be doing?"

"I have my investigator poking around the school, the neighborhood, and Claxton's life. He may be in contact with you both. His name is Ty Hill. I think we are good for now. I'll stay in touch, and if either of you thinks of anything, please get in touch. And Bo, keep your nose clean..."

Chapter 7

February 19, 2022

Like his Preliminary Arraignment, Bo's Preliminary Hearing was scheduled for ten o'clock at Philadelphia's Municipal Court at the Stout Center for Criminal Justice in Philadelphia.

In addition to Melanie Wexler, Bo's immediate family was in attendance, but a few others were in the courtroom. Preliminary Hearings were mostly routine. First, the prosecutor would present one or two witnesses, usually the investigating officer, and offer the minimum amount of evidence to show "probable cause." The defense would then ask for dismissal on the grounds of insufficient evidence. The judge would deny this, and they would move to bail.

At ten o'clock sharp, the bailiff called the court to order, "All rise, court is now in session. The Commonwealth of Pennsylvania vs. the Defendant, Bowman Campbell. The Honorable Judge Emmett P. Ferguson, presiding." Judge Ferguson took a seat and motioned all others to do the same.

He had presided over the Preliminary Arraignment a week ago and, going off script, had allowed House Arrest with electronic monitoring for the past week.

The proceedings began and followed the template. The judge asked the attorneys to identify themselves and asked the prosecution to proceed.

Assistant District Attorney Michelle Pugh called Detective Brown to the stand. He was the only witness and testified as to how the anonymous tip that had been received, the weapon and cocaine found in the defendant's locker, and the arrest at Overbrook High School.

"Care to cross-examine, Ms. Wexler?"

"Briefly, thank you, Your Honor." She stood in place. "Detective, for the court's benefit, do you have Bo Campbell's fingerprints or any DNA on either the weapon, the drugs, or the deceased's body?"

"No."

"Are you aware of any motive Bo Campbell may have had to kill his best friend?"

"No."

"No further questions, Your Honor." Wexler returned to her seat.

The state then rested; confident they had proved their case.

Judge Ferguson then said, "Ms. Wexler, your turn. You may call your first witness."

Melanie stood and admonished, "The defense moves for a dismissal of the charges as the prosecution has failed to prove its case beyond a reasonable doubt, Your Honor." Melanie had no expectations that the judge would agree and had told the Campbells that.

"Motion denied, Ms. Wexler. Do you wish to call your first witness?"

"No thank you, Your Honor, the defense rests."

"The court finds in favor of the prosecution, and I assume you wish to discuss bail, counselors? Ms. Pugh?"

Michelle Pugh stood and said, "Your Honor, the People will restate its position that bail is inappropriate and extremely rare in a murder case. The defendant is an adult and should be treated so, and we request that the bail be rescinded and the defendant is held without bail until the trial. Thank you, Your Honor."

"Ms. Wexler?" Judge Ferguson said, nodding toward Melanie.

"For all the reasons Ms. Campbell stated at the prior hearing, Your Honor, we believe that this situation meets the high standard for the Court to make an exception to grant bail. There is no evidence, nor any motive, nor have the People even told us what murder charge they will be entering. We consider this a bogus, politically motivated prosecution and renew our plea for bail, if not dismissal. Thank you, Your Honor."

Wexler sat down, held her breath and put her hand on Bo's shoulder, who had been sitting motionless through this ordeal.

Judge Ferguson said, "I have already ruled that this matter will not be dismissed, Ms. Wexler, but I remain sympathetic to your appeal for continuing bail. The defendant will remain under House Arrest with electronic monitoring and will be permitted two hours a day for outdoor exercise. He may also leave the house to meet with his counsel, with pre-approval from the court official. He will not be permitted to attend school. I will assume tutoring is available so that the defendant can potentially graduate in June; if that is not the case, we will revisit this matter. We are adjourned."

Chapter 8

October 18, 2018

It may have been Indian Summer, but no one knew exactly what or when it was or if it was even a thing. But whenever the temperature hit sixty-five degrees in October, Indian Summer was all anyone in Philadelphia could talk about.

Such was today! Bo and Carl Watkins were planning to head down to the river drives for a run. When Carl showed up at Bo's house, Bo asked if Carl would mind if he called Sherman to join them.

"I guess not," Carl responded unenthusiastically.

"What, you got a problem with Sherm?"

"Nah! I just thought we might talk about practice. You know, I'm still not sure I'll make the team."

"We can talk about it now and later. You'll make it, Carl. You were the eighth man last year, and you've improved. Now that you are a Junior, the coach will want your experience. I'm thinking you could be the sixth man, maybe even start. How about we go over to Tustin tomorrow and work on some stuff? I think I can set you up for some easy shots."

"Fair enough, Bo. Let's go pick up Sherman."

The river drives were initially the East, and West River Drives, on the respective sides of the Schuylkill River. Thirty years ago, for reasons known only to them, the City Council renamed them the John B. Kelly and M. L. King Drives. Only tourists referred to these new names; residents still called them East and West.

Bo, Sherm, and Carl arrived and parked on the West. Carl asked, "We all good for a loop?" A loop was an eight-and-a-half-mile circle going east past the Art Museum, back out the East River Drive, and crossing the River at the Falls Bridge.

"Good by me," Bo said.

"Me too," added Sherman.

Bo and Carl liked to talk while they ran, and Sherman put in his AirPods to listen to the radio. They took off at about a seven-minute-a-mile pace. Bo asked Sherman, "How's your team look this year?"

Removing one earphone, "We're the team to beat," Sherm quickly replied.

"That so? I was thinking the same thing, bruh. You know, The Brook can't be took!"

"I'm going off hearing and talking, Bruh!" Sherm stated emphatically, ending the discussion.

"OK, Sherm, listen to your music."

An hour later, they were back at the car where they had started, exchanging fist bumps and gasping to catch their breaths. They walked for fifteen minutes, hydrated, toweled off, and headed home.

After dropping Sherman off, Carl said to Bo, "Don't you find Sherman weird?"

"Not sure what you mean, Carl?"

"I don't know, his speech, eyes, facial mannerisms, I can't put my finger on it, the guy seems off to me."

"I don't see it, Carl. I think you have a hard-on about him for some reason. Lighten the F up!"

"Going to church with the folks tomorrow morning. Meet at Tustin at eleven?"

"Make it noon. See you then!"

Chapter 9

December 13, 2018

James McNeil arrived at the Overbrook High Field House at three-thirty, an hour before the scheduled tip-off. Today was Bo's first game as a freshman, and James anticipated a large crowd.

James liked to sit on the last row, center court, believing that gave him the best view of the entire court. He would try to hold six seats for other family members, but they may prefer to sit closer to the front. He texted his wife and daughter to advise them the place was already half full.

Overbrook's Field House was built in the '90s and had a thousand seats. He smiled as he recalled the old gym where Wilt Chamberlain and other legends played. No amount of disinfectant could temper the stench; with standing room, it could only squeeze in about a hundred spectators. While the fieldhouse now showed some wear, it had shaded windows, a parquet floor like the Boston Garden, and eight retractable side court baskets for gym and open play use.

While the seats were still retractable, the back-killing benches had been replaced with much more comfortable plastic seats. Overbrook Panther logos decorated center court and the baselines, and Public League and City Championship banners covered the walls. Both teams completed their shoot-around and returned to the locker rooms. The pep band was tuning up.

Overbrook was playing Central High today and was a heavy favorite. But Bo would be the focus; could he live up to the pre-season hype? Bo seemed fine last night, but no doubt would have butterflies in his tummy about now.

At four-ten, James' wife Linda appeared and joined him. Their daughter and Bo's mom, Winnie, chose to sit with the other players' families. Bo's sister, Claudia, was with her mom. She was an attorney at a small firm in Ardmore after graduating from Law School at Villanova. Bo's brother, Kendrick, was expected after his class at St. Joseph's. Noticeably a no-show was Bo's dad, Hugh. No one could be certain of his plans.

Ten minutes before game time, both teams came onto the court and went through their warm-ups. Trying to replicate the NBA experience, the lights were dimmed with a spotlight on the bench. Central's starting team was announced, then the pep band started playing while the announcer said, "AND FOR YOUR OVERBOOK PANTHERS..." and the Overbrook players were introduced to fanfare and butt bumps.

The players lined up, and play began.

The game was anticlimactic as Overbrook got off to a quick start and fed on that. They led by fifteen at the half and wound up winning by twenty-two points. Bo played his style of game and finished with sixteen points, twelve assists, and fourteen rebounds. He sat out the last five minutes of the game, as did the other starters.

The coach was taking the players to Larry's for steaks and hoagies. James and Linda gathered with the family, and he asked them all to Chili's for dinner. They drove there in two cars, and James asked, "Do we need a seat for Hugh?"

Winnie replied, "Yes, I just spoke to him, and he's on his way."

They got a table for five, and Hugh arrived before they had ordered.

"What I'd miss? Sorry, I couldn't make it." Hugh did not offer any reason for his absence.

James replied, "They won comfortably, and Bo looked great. sixteen, twelve, and fourteen. Sat out last five minutes."

"James, you think he'll need to score more to draw the attention of the big colleges?"

"I don't know for sure, Hugh. You recall that Villanova approached him at Narberth last summer, so I think the local schools will be aware.

But will Duke, North Carolina, Kentucky, and UCLA send scouts? That's anybody's guess, but the kid's a frosh. Plenty of time for that."

In today's world of money in college football and basketball, YouTube posts, social media proliferation, and cellphone cinematography, few great ballplayers got ignored. Bo had plenty of eyes on him.

"Let's order," James suggested.

Back at Larry's, the kids were chowing down. Larry's was originally located a block away from Overbrook High, across the street from Tustin Playground. Ten years ago, they relocated to the St. Joseph's campus, two miles away. They figured St. Joe's had a larger student body and night school, so kids could pick up dinner on the way to class. Larry's was known to be *The Home of the Bellyfiller*, a cheesesteak with a pound of meat, fried onions, and Cheese Wiz. It always ranked high whenever polls were taken for *The Best Cheesesteak in Philly*.

Larry's decor was vintage Formica and vinyl saved only by the pictures of famous athletes who had visited. With only two tables inside, Larry's encouraged take-out like their better-known rivals in South Philly, Pat's and Geno's.

The players seemed to be split fifty-fifty between cheesesteaks and Italian hoagies. Coach Rosen felt the need to make a few remarks.

"Great game, guys! I loved the ball movement, intense defense, and overall team play. It's a long season, but this is a great start to it. Practice tomorrow, and we play Bartram on Thursday at their place. Everyone got a ride home?" he asked.

They all nodded and resumed eating!

Chapter 10

February 16, 2022

"Why didn't we take the subway?" Claudia asked rhetorically.

"Your call, sis!"

"I hate driving into the city. The subway takes eight minutes, and this will take forty-five."

"And you miss that subway atmosphere."

She ignored her brother's comment and said, "Bo, anything you can tell me you withheld from Mr. Chasnoff?"

"Why would you think that?"

"Just a hunch."

Staring at the side of her head, Bo asked, "Are you my sister or my attorney?"

"Both, but sister first and always."

"As my lawyer, you are sworn to secrecy, right? You must swear not to tell a soul."

"Stop the drama, Bo. Out with it."

Bo put his hands into his face, then let out a deep breath as he gathered himself. Peering at Claudia, whose eyes remained on the road, he finally got it out, "Sherman and I... we... we... were more than friends."

"You're kidding me? Who else knows this? Carl? How, when, I need details, and I need them now."

Claudia tried to look shocked, but for some time, she had noticed Bo paid more attention to guys than girls when they were in a crowd, and was more fastidious about his grooming than most jocks. So, while she suspected, she preferred to allow him to come out on his own schedule. She feared she might have even smiled slightly.

"No one, really. Yes, I told Carl, that was more awkward than this. Neither Sherm or I wanted this to affect our basketball lives or future.

Can you appreciate that?" Bo was still hugging himself and looking out the window.

"I can, Bo, but you know Mom and Dad would be totally accepting. How about Jessica?"

"Jessica knows that I am gay, but not about Sherman and me. She may have suspicions. I have encouraged her to see other guys."

"I'm not certain if or how this might impact the case, Bo, but you must share this with Chasnoff."

"Can you do that if or when necessary?" He looked pleadingly at his sister.

Claudia only had a hundred more questions but thought it best to go easy on Bo. The car ride home was quiet. She dropped Bo off and continued to her apartment in Bala Cynwyd, fifteen minutes away, just outside the city.

When Bo entered the house, his mom and dad were waiting, like the jury waiting for the judge to enter the courtroom. "I'll answer all your questions at dinner. I need some alone time right now."

Bo went up to his room and shut the door. Then, he FaceTimed Jessica.

"Yo, Bo, whatta you know?" was Jessica's standard answering line.

"Not as much as you, Jess. Just got back from the lawyer's office. On the way back, I had to tell my sister."

"Tell her what?"

"You know, about my sexuality."

"Really? How'd that go?"

"She's fine, of course, but, and this is a big but, she says I need to tell my attorney. I fear this secret might be slipping out, and I can't stop it. And she's wondering if this might be related to Sherm's death and the frame-up."

"How might it be, Bo?"

"OK, Jess, I know you probably suspected this, but Sherm and I were hooking up. I still have no idea how this might relate to his death."

"Thanks for finally 'fessing. Sherm confided in me a year ago. Snap me after dinner."

Bo's mom had made fried chicken, mashed potatoes, and string beans. Bo's favorite meal. She was treating this like a birthday or his Last Supper. The interrogation went easy, compared to Chasnoff's.

But all Bo could think about was how his relationship with Sherman may have contributed to his death and the frame-up. He knew this question would continue to occupy his mind until he got it, or his trial came first.

Tomorrow, he and his mom had permission from the Court to meet with the principal and discuss if and how he could continue his studies so he could graduate with his class in June. And that minor matter of a trial in May.

And Saturday was Sherman's funeral.

Chapter 11

May 15, 2019

In West Philly, Big Earl Jackson was an out-of-towner. He grew up in Southwest Philly and went to Bartram High. He never graduated, as he decided his career path did not require a diploma.

He started his life of crime on the streets as a runner, but like many runners, he dreamed bigger. He served an apprenticeship with Spade in Southwest. At twenty-eight, Spade was the main man in the Southwest handling a full product line from weed to Oxy to fentanyl and H. Pops Williams was the only other banger of note in the hood, and was only a minor nuisance to Pops.

Jackson stepped in when Spade disappeared thirty years ago. There was harmony for a while, but Pops had big ideas also.

Big Earl moved to West Philly twenty-five years ago when Pops got greedy and began threatening Earl's guys. Some were beaten, and one was killed. Earl considered going to war with Pops, but a lot of people got hurt in war, and Earl considered himself non-violent. He could be tough if he needed to be but felt no need to prove himself daily.

Pops could have easily found him if he wanted to; West and Southwest were almost indistinguishable, but Pops was pleased to be rid of Earl.

It took Earl five years to build his business in West Philly. First, he established runners at the local high schools, West Philly and Overbrook, Greenfield and Penn Alexander Middle Schools, and U of P, Drexel, and Saint Joseph's Universities. In addition, his runners would make student contacts in the schools. Initially, it was weed, but then it progressed and he offered a menu from Crack to Oxy.

He added prostitution and grew from two girls to fifteen. While he oversaw the business side, his cousin Sheila took care of the girls.

Earl thought that 50% of West Philly teenagers lost their virginity with Sheila's girls.

Every business had challenges, and Big Earl's were competition, employee loyalty, supply channels, product quality, and occasionally, the police.

Earl was having lunch today at the Rib Joint with his lieutenant and confidant, Brahim Jones. Jones was primarily focused on distribution and had asked to meet with Earl. No one asked to meet with Earl to discuss the Eagles' draft picks; it was always a problem.

"Brahim, what's on your mind?"

"I got an issue going on at Overbrook; I ain't certain as yet whether it is Spooky or one of his runners. But we're short on cash. I was wondering if you got some ideas, Earl?"

"You mean other than offing Spooky?"

"Yeah, that would be the last resort."

"What's Spooky sayin'?"

"Not much. Said he'd watch the kids closer."

"You tell Spooky that we met, and he's got two weeks to clean up his act. If not, you send a message. Got it?" Earl said, making a gun with his fingers.

Chapter 12

October 12, 2019

Basketball try-outs and practice had begun. Having won the City Championship last year, the expectations were at least for the same this year, and Overbrook would have targets on their backs as everyone wanted to upset the Champs.

Bo had been named first-team All-Public and second-team All-City. He received feelers from Villanova and Temple locally, and former Villanova star Ed Pickney was in touch with him from Texas. Bo played in the Narberth League in the summer but skipped the Tustin League in favor of a couple of AAU games. He had grown another inch, and his game continued progressing.

But Bo had one problem.

Jessica Marks!

Since meeting Jessica the prior summer, they had become good friends. Going to different schools, they did not see each other much during the week, but they were usually together on Friday or Saturday nights. They would go to friends' houses for group hangouts, chilled in Suburban Square in Ardmore, or just stayed home and watched TV or play Xbox. Carl Watkins would often join them, and occasionally Sherman Claxton.

But last weekend, Jessica went for a full, open-mouth kiss rather than their usual peck on the cheek. It was immediately apparent to both that this was unexpected, and Bo was uncomfortable. They did not speak about it, but no doubt they would have to, and this was Bo's problem. He liked Jessica a lot, trusted her, and felt comfortable confiding in her. But he was not attracted to her. He knew she was cute, perhaps even hot, and his friends all thought they were hooking up. So, what was the problem?

As they usually did, Carl and Bo walked home together after practice.

Carl asked, "Think I'll start this year?"

"Absolutely, your time is now, bruh!"

"You think we are as good as last year? We'll miss Dwight."

"We will miss Dwight, but I think Lamont will fill the void, and we all need to step up."

"Any idea what's going on with Big Mac? He seems to have a hard-on for everyone and everything. Can't make the guy happy."

Reggie McIntosh was the Assistant Coach and was a tough taskmaster. Coach Rosen often allowed Big Mac to run the practices. The players assumed that Big Mac was vying for Rosen's job, as there was speculation that Coach was getting offers from college teams.

"I don't even try! In one ear, out the other. Don't let him get to you."

"You and Jessica got plans for the weekend?"

"We talked about going out to King of Prussia Mall if we can get a ride. You game?"

"Definitely! I think I can get my mom to drive us out. Can you or Jess get us back?"

"Think so. While we are on the subject, you think Jessica is pretty hot, don't you?"

"She's a dime, bruh!"

"I love Jessica for sure, but as a friend, and she wants more, that whole romance kind of thing."

"You telling me you don't want that? What's wrong with you, man? I'd be glad to pinch-hit for you."

"I'm not certain Annette would go for that, bruh. I gotta tell her something."

"Whatever you do, don't tell her the truth. Girls can't handle the truth. Make something up like you got kicked in the balls and can't get it up, or you're gay, or how about you're saving yourself for marriage?"

"You're a big help, Carl. See you tomorrow." Bo gave him an eye roll.

Chapter 13

February 19, 2022

A typical winter day in Philadelphia; it was bitterly cold and overcast the morning of Sherman Claxton's funeral. The wind added to the discomfort level. Despite the forecast, it felt like snow was in the air.

Claudia picked up Bo at nine-thirty, and they drove to the United Memorial Gospel Church at 59th and Delancey Streets. Bo had received the approval of the court to attend. They had to park a block away, and a crowd was in line outside the small church. As to be expected, there were a lot of Sherman's West Philly and Widener classmates, faculty, friends, and family.

They joined the queue outside. They were glad they had dressed for the cold. Claudia had on a pantsuit, a mid-length black wool coat, gloves, and a wool scarf she also used to cover her ears. Bo was more casual but neat with slacks, a sweater, a parka, and a black and orange ski cap pulled over his ears. His Air-Jordans were non-negotiable.

Bo asked his sister, "What happens here? I've never been to a funeral."

"Only been to two myself, but typically, the casket will be open, and this line will walk to the front of the church, pay respects to the family, and then say goodbye to Sherman. Then there will be a church service, a procession out to Laurel Hill Cemetery, and many will return to the Claxton residence. It will be very emotional, Bo, so do not be afraid to cry."

"No way I can see the family or Sherman. I'll pay my respects at the house later, OK?"

"Your call, Bo, but play it by ear. You may feel differently when we get in there."

This neighborhood had seen too many of its youth get killed, but the funerals were always personal and emotional. The minister knew the Claxton family well, and Bo's father made an uncomfortable attempt at a eulogy. There were few, if any, dry eyes, including Bo's.

The burial was at the Laurel Hill Cemetery. At the cemetery, Bo and Claudia recognized Detective Brown and his partner hanging in the back. Bo did not know if they were watching him or looking for someone else in the crowd.

It would be twelve-forty-five before they got back to the Claxton home at 53rd and Osage Streets. The small house was crowded, with food and liquor in the dining room. Some were openly crying, others talking about the good times, Sherman's basketball exploits, and his fun-loving personality. Sherman's parents and grandparents sat in the living room, receiving condolences but aching in their grief.

Everyone in the house knew Bo, if not personally, through reputation. Bo could feel their eyes on him, most wondering what Sherman's alleged killer was doing here. Bo knew he had to speak with Sherm's mom and dad, but what could he say, and how would they receive him? Sherman's mom, Coralie Claxton, was making no effort to hide her grief, and at times her wailing could be heard throughout the tiny house. Claudia held onto Bo, sensing his need for support. They approached the Claxtons. Sherman's mother saw them at once, stood, and stepped toward Bo with her arms open, and embraced him.

"Oh, Bo! We are so glad you are here!"

Bo was unable to speak, in full crying mode. Sherman's dad had joined in the group hug. Claudia introduced herself, and the four stood there, sharing their grief.

Finally, wiping his tears, Bo mumbled, "You have to know I did not do this. I can't tell you how sorry I am."

"We know Bo, and we told the police that there was no way you could have harmed Sherman. Please have something to eat. We'll talk again, if not today, perhaps you can visit later in the week."

"Will do, Mr. and Mrs. Claxton, and thank you for believing me."

Claudia and Bo moved away, picked up a cookie, and exited.

Chapter 14

March 10, 2020

Overbrook had again won the City Championship with only one loss during the season. Bo had to sit out for two weeks in January with a groin pull, and they went 3-1 in that period.

They had advanced to the PIAA AAAA State Championship in Hershey, two hours west of Philadelphia, where they lost a close game to Uniontown High, 68-65. Bo had been limited to fifteen points, well below his season average of twenty-two points per game. Worse, he missed a three-point attempt at the buzzer, which would have sent the game into overtime. Bo took the loss personally and apologized to the team and coaches. Coach Rosen reminded them that they won as a team and lost as a team and that they would not have been there if not for Bo's playing and leadership.

That didn't help.

The players took the bus home from Hershey, but the Campbell contingent still needed two cars. Hugh Campbell drove his wife, son, and daughter, while James McNeil drove his wife Linda, Jessica Marks, and Sherman Claxton.

They all agreed, wait until next year.

Bo took the week off from playing but agreed to meet Sherman at Haddington Recreation Center the following Saturday. The gym opened on Saturdays in the winter for basketball, and they could find a pick-up game there. Sherman's High School career ended, and he accepted a scholarship offer from Widener University in suburban Philadelphia. That would keep him close enough to Philly for his family to attend games but far enough away that he was not expected home for dinner every night.

At Haddington, Bo and Sherm won their first game but lost the second. They decided they had had enough rather than wait for another game. They walked over to Mickey Ds for lunch. The place was quiet, and after they unwrapped their burgers, Sherman got serious.

"We need to talk, bruh."

"No one needs to talk, Sherm. You mean you want to talk, which is rarely good. What's up?"

Sherman leaned in to within six inches of Bo's face, looking over his shoulder in both directions to make certain no one else could hear, "Whatever! I'm not sure how you will take this, but I need you to know that I am gay."

With a mouthful of fries, Bo looked up. "You're what?"

"You heard me. I'm gay."

"When the hell did that happen?"

"I've known it for a couple of years, Bo. At first, I wanted to deny it. I even fooled around with a couple of girls to see if I might get over it. But I am who I am. I like guys."

Bo was aware of gay people, but never knew any personally, until now. He wondered how that happened, and what it was like. And why did Sherm feel the need to tell him? He would soon get that answer.

"I got to tell you Sherm, I'm shocked. But it doesn't change anything with us, I hope. We're still friends, right?

"Of course, but that's not all, Bo. I have seen you and Jessica together, and you're not hookin' up. Anything you want to tell me?"

"You think I'm gay because Jessica and I aren't getting it on?"

"Hey, if I'm wrong, I'm wrong. No offense intended. I just thought we should have this conversation. I'll be off to Widener in the fall, so I thought I needed to tell you this now. We good?"

"Always, Sherm."

But this conversation would change Bo's life, and, as they each went their own way home, Bo could think of nothing else.

Chapter 15

March 13, 2020

Lincoln McNeil was the patriarch of the McNeil family.

He had lived all his 89 years in West Philadelphia. The neighborhood had changed over the years; long gone were the days when it was only Blacks and Jews. The Jews had moved to Wynnefield and Overbrook, then off to Penn Valley, but gentrification had gone OK for West Philly; the Blacks and Asians had a mostly peaceful co-existence. And with the expansion of the Drexel and Penn campuses, even some white professors and students lived on the fringes.

McNeil had been in the record business, and Dick Clark once referred to him as one of the key players in creating the Philly Sound back in the '60s. Then, in the '80s, he formed Philly Beats, a production company that provided music to the movie and TV industry when filming in Philadelphia. His grandson, Rasheed, ran the business today.

Weather permitting, he walked over to 52nd & Chestnut Streets, bought the *Philadelphia Daily News*, and read it with a cup of coffee at the Dunkin' Donuts. Once a week, he allowed himself a glazed donut with rainbow jimmies. That's where he was today, meeting with his son, James.

"Yo Pops, over here!" James called. He stood and hugged his dad.

"How you doing, James? Did Bo get over the loss yet?"

"Yeah, he's OK, Pops. Kids move on rather quickly, not like us old guys."

"And all good over at Philly Beats?"

"Why you asking? You haven't been over there yet today?"

"Funny man! I'm not sure Rasheed would tell me if he was having any problems."

"But I would, so relax."

"And what you got going on today?"

"Nada, but me and the guys got a gig tonight over at the Rainbow Lounge. Maybe I could have Linda bring you over for the first set?"

"That would be nice, thanks."

They leisurely drank their coffee talking about the 76ers' chances in the playoffs, and how serious this COVID thing in China might be.

After turning over the business to Rasheed, James was able to pursue his passion, his jazz quartet, the SoundMachine. James played sax and sang. His buddies Duke, Lamont, and "Snare" played trumpet, piano, and drums, respectively. But, of course, they all sang.

They had a regular gig on Fridays and Saturdays at The Jazz Corner on the Penn campus and filled in the week playing other venues. They had a nice following in the Delaware Valley and could get more work, but the guys were all fine with their schedule. Carl and Snare had day jobs, and Lamont had a disability pension from the Marines. James, of course, would go and hang around Philly Beats and make suggestions his son occasionally welcomed.

"OK then, Pops, see you tonight, and be careful walking home."

Chapter 16

March 3, 2022

Claudia and Bo were meeting again at Fred Chasnoff's downtown office. Claudia had asked for the meeting after Bo came out of the closet. Chasnoff omitted his suit coat, but otherwise dressed identically to their last visit.

"Claudia, Bo, what's on your minds?"

Claudia looked to Bo who was unable to hold eye contact, or speak. After a pregnant pause, Claudia answered, "Fred, Bo told me something the other day that you need to know. He's been sitting on it for a couple of years now. Bo is gay, and he and Claxton were in a relationship."

"Whoa! Why didn't you share that at our last meeting, Bo?"

Bo sat wringing his hands, shifted in his chair, and replied, "No one else knows, Mr. Chasnoff. Sherman and I said we would keep this a secret until we were both off to college. We both thought it might affect any basketball scholarships."

"When did this relationship begin, Bo?"

"July 2019."

"Bo, my experience is that secrets are never quite as secret as the keepers would like. Secondly, and much more relevant to our case, this is now a motive. I am already thinking that the DA might have this information."

"Why would this be a motive, Mr. Chasnoff? Sherman and I loved each other."

"You know that Bo, and I believe you, but with the planted evidence, the DA will claim you had a lover's quarrel, falling out, or one of you was cheating on the other. They, of course, don't need the truth, but it will fit the narrative they will construct."

Claudia asked, "Just how do we deal with this?"

"I'm not certain we do, but Bo, you must assume that this will come out no later than the trial, but more likely, before. You may want to discuss this with your parents and some of your better friends. Our defense will need to change now rather than saying there was no motive for you to kill Sherman. We'll have to prove either the evidence was planted or, preferably, construct our narrative around who else may have wanted Claxton dead."

"Shit! Mom and Dad will freak! And school will be a real shitshow! How did this mess get started?"

"That is the key question, Bo, and one we must find out before May. Anything else for now?"

"I think we are good, Fred. Thanks for squeezing us in," Claudia said.

Before they even got on the elevator, Bo tugged her sister's arm and pleaded, "Please be with me when I tell Mom and Dad."

Looking up at her foot taller brother, "Will do. I'm having them over to my place for Sunday dinner. Tell them I invited you. They may be shocked, Bo, but you know they will quickly accept. They may even know or suspect already. You heard what Chasnoff said about secrets."

Chapter 17

March 23, 2022

Detective Vernon Brown arrived at the Jazz Corner at seven. He was meeting James McNeil there before James began playing at eight. They met in the lobby, and James led them to a table.

"How about grabbing a bite?"

"I'm in! What's going on, James?"

"Samo, samo, bruh! Anything new with the case?"

"And here I thought you asked me down here out of pure love."

"That too, Vern. Do you have any motive for Bo killing Sherman?"

"We think we do, James, but I cannot share that with you yet. It could be sensitive, and if true, it would be better if you don't hear it from me."

"Then why you here, Vern?"

"To visit with a friend and listen to some good music. You intending to play any?"

"We'll try!"

Chapter 18

March 22, 2020

Lincoln McNeil was having his morning coffee at the Dunkin' Donuts. He needed to be home by nine-thirty for his therapy. A lifelong smoker, McNeil got respiratory treatment three times a week and needed to sleep with a C-PAP mask.

He left the Dunkin' at nine-twenty and joined the queue waiting to cross 52nd Street. Rush hour hadn't ended yet, and a dozen commuters waited on the sidewalk. Anticipating the light change, the herd inched ahead. McNeil led the charge, but suddenly he stumbled forward, and a black SUV appeared. It did not slow down but sped up. It hit McNeil, going about forty MPH, thrusting him six feet in the air. Rather than stop, the SUV accelerated, made a left on Ranstead, and was gone.

Lincoln McNeil was clinging to life when he was brought into the ER at the University of Pennsylvania Hospital. His breathing was shallow, and his pulse was weak. There was no external bleeding, but who knew what was happening inside?

While the ER staff were hooking up oxygen, an IV for anesthesia, monitors, and other tools of life maintenance, McNeil went into cardiac arrest. With no time to spare, the attending Intern applied the paddles in an attempt to restore the heartbeat. Unfortunately, after a minute, it was clear they had lost him. He was pronounced dead at ten-ten on March twenty-second.

Back on 52nd Street, Detectives Vernon Brown and Chuck Jankowski had interviewed seven bystanders; two had a similar recollection of a man about six-foot tall wearing a gray hoodie standing behind McNeil. Was he trying to scoot past McNeil, or did he shove him? Neither could be sure. Neither had seen his face nor that he had disappeared in the chaotic seconds after McNeil had been struck.

James McNeil had agreed to meet Detectives Brown and Jankowski and the 18th Police District station at 55th and Pine. When he arrived, the Desk Captain called, and Jankowski escorted McNeil to interview room number three. The 55th and Pine station was now the oldest police station in the city, and it looked it. Peeling green concrete walls, tile floors, and metal desks; it was depressing. They were planning its one-hundredth birthday celebration in two years if it did not crumble before then. No one was buying balloons just yet.

Introductions were made, seats were selected, and it was time to get down to business.

Brown started, "I met your dad many years ago. When I was new on patrol, I stopped at PhillyBeats as I loved music. I thought I would introduce myself as the new guy in the Hood, and your dad started telling me about the heydays of music in the city, the '60s, and '70s, the Uptown theater shows. I couldn't get him to stop even if I wanted to, but I didn't. He sure could tell a story."

"Yeah, that was my dad. He was still telling those same stories to anyone who might listen. You'd think the Earth revolved around the Four Tops and The Temptations. I gotta tell you, Officer, you look familiar to me. Where'd you go to school?"

"Just down the street at West Philly, Class of 1977."

"That must be it, West Philly Class of 1974," fist-pumping to himself.

"Oh wow, we ought to talk sometime, but my partner looks like he's falling asleep. So, you West Catholic guys don't want to listen to us Publics reminisce?"

Jankowski yawned saying, "Oh no, I'm loving this old Homie revival. Why don't I go out for lunch, maybe dinner? Then, call me when you're done."

"OK, OK, Jank, let's put the tape on."

"We are sorry about your dad. This appears to be a murder rather than a simple hit-and-run. The witnesses said the car sped up to hit your dad deliberately, and one of them was certain your dad had been pushed off the curb. Unfortunately, we've got no good video of either the driver or the pusher and no luck yet tracing the car. Do you have any thoughts about who might want your father dead?"

"I do not. My dad has led a rather quiet life since retiring. Free Donut Day for Veterans at Dunkin' was the highlight of his week. I spoke with my dad's best bud, who mentioned he had been gambling heavily. I knew my dad was comfortable financially, but apparently, he was cash-poor with a lot of his money tied up and in trusts for his grandkids. The friend thought he might have gotten a loan from Big Earl. He was going to talk to Earl."

Brown smiled at hearing Earl's name. "Big Earl, really? The American Dream. Take your profits from drugs and prostitution and loan shark it out at 30% interest rates. Does your friend have a name?"

James looked up, shaking his head in the negative, "I'd rather not say if it's all the same to you. He and I thought we would do some investigating on our own. There are guys here in the Hood that will never talk to you, nothing personal. If we come up with anything, we'll let you know."

Brown made a half-hearted plea, "Not a good idea, but I'm sure I won't talk you out of it. Be careful. Big Earl is an enemy you don't want. I'll call you about catching up on West Philly memories."

"Hey, why not come by the Jazz Corner Friday night? Me and my guys got a gig there Friday and Saturday nights. We can chat during our break."

"Might do that. I'll let you know. Also, my wife might want to come and defend Overbrook High. Thanks again for coming to the station."

Chapter 19

March 5, 2022

Claudia Campbell lived in a new apartment building in Bala Cynwyd, located on the suburban side of City Avenue, which separated it from the city of Philadelphia. Most of the new construction in Bala over the last thirty years had been office buildings where businesses and individuals located to avoid Philadelphia city taxes and crime. They still avoided the city tax, but crime, not so much.

Several new, modern apartment buildings had sprouted up in the last ten years, providing comfortable accommodations for the aging population abandoning their large homes in the suburbs. But, of course, it was also a great place for the affluent Millennials and GenZers who chose not to live downtown.

Claudia moved here eighteen months ago, the first in her family to abandon West Philadelphia. She caught some grief for that, but she reminded her parents she was only ten minutes away from the old Hood.

Her parents, along with Bo, and Jessica, arrived promptly at five-thirty. Bo and Claudia had agreed that including Jessica would provide a good buffer. The family were all meat eaters, so she prepared a flank steak with her mom's marinade recipe, mashed potatoes, and collard greens. She cheated and bought an apple pie for dessert from Acme.

They sat in the living area, and Claudia got everyone drinks to go along with the cheese plate and cashews she had set out. Diet Pepsi for you kids?

"Claudia, to what do we owe this honor?" Hugh finally inquired.

"Do I need a reason to have my family over for dinner?"

"Since this is only the second time we have been here for dinner, I would have to say yes."

"Nailed again. Bo, this is your show."

All eyes turned to the stone-cold Bo, who suddenly felt the need to uncross his huge legs and straighten up in his chair. "Mom and Dad, I've got something I need to tell y'all...OK, just let me get this out... I'm gay and was in a relationship with Sherman."

Silence!

Hugh and Winnie stared at Bo. Jessica and Claudia stared at Hugh and Winnie. Bo stared at the ceiling, relieved that he had gotten the words out, but still waiting for a response. No one was certain who would speak first, or what they might say. Then, finally, Winnie spoke up.

"Bo, honey, your dad and I are not shocked and had discussed it after Sherman was killed. We love you, and nothing will change that. Is that all?"

But Hugh added quickly, "Just how might this affect your trial? Have you discussed it with Chasnoff?"

Claudia took that one, "We have, and one of the reasons we wanted to tell you now is he feels it will come out at the trial, if not before. He says it gives Bo a motive for killing Sherman, some problem with the relationship."

"Is that true, Bo? Was something going on with you and Sherman?"

"No, not at all. But Mr. Chasnoff says it doesn't matter. The prosecutor will present it as if it were true, and of course, it will be difficult for us to refute."

"This is a lot for you to have to deal with, Bo. Are you OK?" his mom asked.

"Not really. I'm scared shitless and, at the same time, missing Sherman like you wouldn't believe."

"Jessica, you've been quiet. What do you think?" Claudia asked, wanting to allow Jessica to take part in the discussion.

"Thanks for asking, Claudia, but I have little to add. I have known about Bo and Sherman for some time. Bo is a great friend, and nothing will ever change that. But, like all of you, the impact on his defense is concerning. But we'll get through it. I'm the optimist who believes that the truth will win the day."

"Second drink, anyone?" Claudia interjected.

They all opted for one!

Chapter 20

April 15, 2020

Big Earl no longer spent much time on the streets but met weekly with his five senior partners. They met in a private room at the Rib Joint at 48th and Spruce tonight. Clyde Webster always took care of them and made the best ribs on this side of Market Street.

With almost every retail establishment in the city closed due to the COVID-19 outbreak, Clyde had opened just for Big Earl's small gathering. They all took precautions and wore masks. They expected this crisis to end in another week or two.

Like every week, the partners expressed concern about the supply channels. Demand was constantly increasing, and he had competition. Earl had the supply connections but needed to add more as the demand exceeded the suppliers' capacity.

The meeting adjourned at about eleven-thirty; they man-hugged outside, and the guys took off as Earl remained and lit a cigarette. He stood there for a couple of minutes, debriefing the meeting in his head. He had parked, as usual, across the street in the church's parking lot; no one was praying at this hour. About ten feet from his car, a man with a ski mask appeared, took aim, and calmly put two rounds in Big Earl. He used a silencer, so there was a good chance Earl would not be found until tomorrow morning.

While the city might be closed, murderers took no vacation. Detectives Brown and Jankowski were on the scene at Bright Hope Baptist Church the next morning. The Desk Sergeant awakened them at six-thirty upon getting the call about a body at the church. They learned it was Big Earl when they were en route.

Of course, the news vans were all there; Action News and KYW were reporting live even though they knew absolutely nothing, including the deceased's identity. No need to let the lack of facts get in the way of a good story. If they were lucky, they could get their viewers an actual shot of real blood.

A few days later, "Hey, Jank," said Detective Brown. "Ballistics got a hit on the gun that was used in Big Earl's murder, claims it is the same gun used in a murder in South Philly."

"We think Big Earl's murder wasn't related to any drug war in West Philadelphia. My brain is about to burst, Vern. I think we need someone smarter than you and me on this."

"Where does this leave the power void in the West Philly drug world?"

"Yet to be determined," Jank guessed.

Chapter 21

March 8, 2022

Philadelphia District Attorney David Kasper had asked his Assistant DA, Michelle Pugh, to arrange this meeting with the investigating detectives.

The Philadelphia DA was an elected position, and in Philadelphia, that almost always meant it was a Democrat. Kasper was now in his second term and, in an almost impossible situation, generally was getting good grades. He was tough on major crimes but did not want to clog the system with much bullshit. Minor drug charges for use or possession, shoplifting, vagrancy, and some assaults were given probation. If they became second or third-time offenders, his team would deal with them more harshly.

Detectives Vernon Brown and Roberta Rumson joined Kasper and Pugh in the DA's office, and they were not certain what to expect. They had been working the case with Pugh, so for the DA to get involved at this point was unusual.

Kasper started, "Thanks for arranging this meeting, Michelle. Vern and Roberta, thanks for being available on short notice. I wanted to make certain we were all on the same page on this case. There have been some reports that we have been too quick to arrest Bo Campbell due to his high-profile. Am I the only one concerned about our evidence?"

Vernon Brown responded first, "I believe you all know that I am a close friend of James McNeil, Bo Campbell's grandfather. I honestly want the kid to be innocent, but with the evidence we have, we and Michelle believed we had sufficient evidence to arrest. But truth be told, the only evidence we have came from an anonymous source. Unless we can confirm it, our case may be weak. I am certain their defense will be that the gun and cocaine were planted in his locker."

"And, if they disprove either the locker evidence, the case is dead in the water," added Rumson.

"Michelle, you have to try the case. What do you think?"

"I think we need to find either additional evidence or make certain what we have is rock solid. And I know Vern and Roberta are chasing these angles. We could not win with the press, Dave. If we had not arrested Campbell, they'd say he was getting preferential treatment."

"I agree, so let's hope we can lock this down before May. Thanks all!"

Chapter 22

April 10, 2020

Overbrook High Coach Myron Rosen grew up in the Northeast section of Philadelphia and attended Central High School. He started for Central in his Junior and Senior years and played well enough to get a partial scholarship to Lehigh University.

But as a 6'2" white guy, he knew his future in the game was limited. But he loved the game, and coaching was a way to stay involved. So, after graduating from Lehigh, he accepted a teaching and assistant coaching position at Souderton High School in the Philly suburbs.

After marrying his college sweetheart, Rosen accepted the Head Coaching position at Harriton High School, and they moved to Havertown, Pennsylvania.

In 2014, he was offered the coaching position at Overbrook High, and for anyone in the Philadelphia and surrounding area, this was the ultimate opportunity in coaching at the high school level. Dating back to the 1950s, Overbrook had sent dozens of its players to play at local and national colleges and a dozen more to the NBA and Europe. The legacy of Wilt Chamberlain was huge on the Overbrook campus, literally and figuratively.

Rosen was now forty, had two kids, and had gained a reputation as a solid, winning coach. A couple of colleges had approached him about their programs. Rosen was sensing that this could be the time to either fish or cut bait, move into the college ranks, or remain a high school coach for the duration. He could hope and expect a couple more good years at the Brook with Bo Campbell, but this might be the time to leverage this success.

He had received a solid offer to coach at Swarthmore College. It was not exactly the ACC, or even The Big Five, but it would be a move up, and would not require relocation. He and his wife Cindy had discussed it and agreed to discuss it again. Swarthmore had requested a decision within ten days.

Rosen was a loyal guy and felt he owed Overbrook for the opportunity they had given him. He considered his players, past and present, a part of his extended family. Who would succeed him here? He was certain that Big Mac would expect consideration, but Rosen was not certain of his assistant coach. This was not his problem he knew, but it still concerned him.

At Overbrook, the Vice Principal, Luther Washington, functioned as the Athletic Director. Rosen considered Luther a good friend and had discussed the Swarthmore offer with him. They were meeting today via Zoom as the Philadelphia schools were closed and all classes were being conducted remotely.

"Can you see and hear me OK, Myron?"

"All is good, Luther. You and the family all OK?"

"So far, thanks. I won't keep you long, but have you made a decision yet?

"Cindy and I have discussed it, but no decision yet. You know I love what we have here Luther."

"We love having you here, but I also respect your career and family come first. I wanted to talk to you today as we have had a complaint about Reggie McIntosh."

"Bad language again?"

"I wish it were only that, Myron. He called one of the kids a no-good faggot."

"Oh shit! Which kid?"

"Not important, Myron. You know why they call it 'Political Correctness?' Because it is correct, and we do not tolerate this from the kids, let alone the faculty and staff. Give him one warning but make certain he knows it is the first and last. You OK doing that, or prefer I handle it?"

"It comes with the job, right? I'll call him. Are you hearing anything about when school might resume?"

"I haven't, Myron. There's some thinking the government is bullshitting us all, and this is much more serious and long-lasting than they are admitting. Principal Phelps said he would not be shocked if school would not resume until the fall."

"Please don't say that, Luther. Most of my players expect to play in the Narberth league this summer."

"Will they play with masks on, Myron, and no touching? I think the Narberth League is the least of our problems. We'll stay in touch and pray this is over sooner than later. Stay safe, Myron."

"Will do, Luther. You and your family also."

Chapter 23

April 8, 2020

Big Earl's death left a void in the drug subculture in West Philadelphia. It was a void that several wannabes were anxious to fill.

After Earl's funeral, his cousin Sheila Gates and Brahim Jones sat on a bench at Laurel Hill Cemetery.

"The police are saying Earl's death had nothing to do with our business but somehow related to a couple of other hits in West and South Philly. Make any sense to you, Sheila?"

"None at all, Heem, but what happens now?"

"I'm thinking you and I run the show now. You OK being partners? I know our suppliers and runners. We need to tighten that up, and you can help."

"Absolutely, Heem. The girls are pretty much independent, but Candy is ready to step up. She can oversee the daily routines, scheduling, and stuff, and I'll still be involved with the money. But we'll be fine there."

"With the schools closed with this COVID shit, we ain't able to move stuff in the schools. I'm not sure where the kids will hang out. People still need their stuff, right? But there's nowhere for them to go to hang out. We gotta have our boys calling their customers and arranging meets. But business will be off for sure. Hope this thing gets fixed real soon. How about the girls?"

"We are doing what we can to keep them safe, and the hope is people still want to have some fun. But we just don't know, Heem."

"It is important we spread the word. I had spoken with Earl about a potential problem at Overbrook. We got competition there, and they might think we are weak. I gotta deal with it when school resumes."

"And my uncle mentioned his concern that Pops Williams from Southwest might be looking to expand. Could we be getting into turf wars, Heem? I ain't prepared for that."

"Too soon to tell, Sheila. It's a real possibility, so we need to push hard. I don't want no war either, but I also don't want to give up what we have built here."

"OK, Heem! I gotta get back to the house. Let's be in touch!"

"Gotcha, sista!"

Back on 52nd Street, Mr. B was talking with Jason Rogers. Not being able to find any place open, they were sitting in Mr. B's car.

Mr. B was a wannabe drug lord; he knew about the workings from his time on the streets. But his employment situation demanded that he remain anonymous, and he was fortunate to make an arrangement with Jason Rogers when the kid dropped out of school three years ago. Mr. B intended to be patient knowing this was still the late Earl's turf for now, but one never knew the future. JRo had one kid, Garrett Green running at Overbrook.

"How's everything out on the streets, JRo?"

"Before this COVID thing, I was thinking we could expand at Overbrook. Now I'm not certain how to do that."

"For sure, J, but with Big Earl gone, and hopefully very soon, COVID, I think it is time to expand into some of the other schools, starting at West Philly. You feeling pretty good that this Bridges dude is ready to be with us on a full-time basis?"

"I think so, B, but he's gonna take a pay cut until we get distribution up to where he is with Earl's team. Any clue who's taking over for Earl?"

"I'm thinking it's gotta be Brahim Jones. We need another runner at Overbrook, pick up two or three at West Philly, and then move on to the other schools. I've already talked to suppliers about our plans. I'll let them know we are expanding and not looking to cut out Earl's guys."

"You got it, B."

"And do I need to remind you, J, that absolutely no one is to hear my name associated in any way with our business? You are the only one who knows of my identity, and it must stay that way, *capisce*?"

"*Capisce*, boss. Loud and clear!"

Chapter 24

March 10, 2022

James McNeil closed his eyes and rested his forehead on the steering wheel. He was feeling helpless, unable to help his grandson. He knew that Bo would never have murdered anyone, let alone Sherman Claxton. And as he learned when his father was murdered, you cannot always stand around waiting for the cops to solve things. It was time he started doing some investigating of his own.

He was parked outside the 59th Street student exit at Overbrook High. He got out of his car and stood, watching for Carl Watkins, Bo's lifelong friend. While James attended Overbrook's rival West Philly High many years ago, the two schools were so close that much of the student body knew each other. James suspected that drugs were the underlying culprit in the Claxton murder *and* Bo's frame-up. He knew little to nothing about the drug culture, and while he prayed Carl and Bo were not involved with it, he thought Carl was a place to start.

At exactly three-fifteen, the kids poured out of the school. Some things hadn't changed much; some of the kids immediately lit cigarettes, and others had their arms around their girlfriends. But not all was the same; a couple of the girls were obviously pregnant, and the kids looked so much older than he did at that same age. It must have been the makeup and clothes.

James got out of the car, not wanting to miss Carl, assuming in fact that Carl was somewhere in this crowd. Finally, James spotted Carl walking alone toward him wearing an Overbrook jacket, jeans, 76ers cap, and untied Air Jordans.

"Yo, Carl! Mr. McNeil here."

Carl stopped, trying to place the face, "Oh, hi, Mr. McNeil. What are you doing here?"

"Waiting for you. How about a ride home?"

"That would be cool."

"My car is this way," leading Carl toward his black Lexus RX350. "You always the last one out of the school?"

"Usually, what's the hurry?"

Once they were both belted up and set to pull off, James asked, "Carl, what can you tell me about the drug world here at Overbrook? Somehow, it has to relate to Sherman's death."

"I can't tell you much, Mr. McNeil, except me and Bo ain't doing any."

"How about Sherman?"

"I don't know Sherm as well, obviously, but I don't think so."

"Did you know about Bo and Sherm?"

"You mean they gay? Yeah, Bo told me about a year ago."

"Anyone else know?"

"Just Jessica. Bo and Sherm were serious about keeping the secret."

"What can you tell me about drugs in school?" As they drove over the 59th Street bridge over the railroad tracks and the old Acme Bakery facility.

"All that I know is there are two dudes that can get you just about anything, weed, crack, Oxy, china white, you name it. I don't know who the source might be. There could be other dudes, too. That's about all I know."

"And who are these dudes?"

"Spooky Little and Spanky Waters," looking around as if someone in the car next to them may be reading his lips.

"How does it work?"

"I think they got a group snap offering bananas, but everyone knows bananas is code for drugs. They meet up with you and get what you want. Nothing happens in school. They make arrangements to meet over at the water ice stand or Tustin Playground. That's all I know, Mr. McNeil. But Sherman was at Widener after graduating from West Philly, so I don't know how these guys got involved with him."

"Last question, is Officer Armstrong still on Security in school?"

"Yep, old Quick Draw."

"This is all very helpful, Carl. I appreciate this. It's a start, anyhow. Give my best to your mom and dad."

"Will do, Mr. McNeil, and thanks for the ride home."

It was a start, but it could be a long story. James thought the next step might be a chat with Quick Draw.

Chapter 25

April 13, 2020

The drug problem in Philly used to be uncomplicated back in the 80s and 90s. Everyone did weed, the rich added heroin, and the poor did crack. Distribution was controlled by the Mob and was regionalized.

Not so today. Was it the glamorization of Crystal Meth, the widespread availability of opioids, increasing consumer demand, or a whole bunch of societal issues? Yes, all of the above.

Fentanyl has become the drug du jour. Fentanyl is a synthetic opioid thirty to fifty times more potent than morphine and is most frequently used legally for post-op pain management. Illegally, China Girl, one of a dozen or so street names, is often mixed with other illegal drugs such as heroin, cocaine, meth, and Molly. Feel free to inhale, inject, eye drop it, or use it in pill form. Because of the fast-acting effect of fentanyl, it is often diluted to provide a cheaper alternative.

Quality control is rather lax; the consumer can never be certain what they are buying.

The Kensington section of Philadelphia has become reputed nationally as the "Tranq Capital of the World." Tranq is a hybrid of fentanyl cut with the animal tranquilizer xylazine. This delightful combination can produce large open wounds where often you can smell the skin rotting and may result in amputation.

Something this great cannot be kept a secret, and the subway line in Philadelphia runs from Kensington in the Northeast out to West Philadelphia. Everyone wants to know where they can get some Tranq.

When he was alive, Big Earl always wanted to give the customers what they demanded. Thus, he established a supply line for Tranq. Well diluted, he was able to offer an eyedropper for $10. Brahim Jones' first call after Earl's death was to "Little Nicky" Scarpatti, the Tranq kingpin in Philadelphia. Scarpatti assured Heem he was still able to meet the demand from his little kitchen on Fisher Point in New Jersey, a short ferry ride across the Delaware to Kensington.

Mr. B and JRo were also using Little Nicky for Tranq, but today, JRo was moving forward with his plan to recruit Dwight Bridges away from Raheem Jones.

Dwight Bridges agreed to meet with Jason Rogers after school at the 49 Stop Food Market, a block away from West Philadelphia High School. Bridges was a Junior at West Philly. He was wearing an Eagles sweatshirt, jeans, red Converse sneakers, and an Adidas cap on backward. He had been running drugs for 18 months now for Damian Mitchell, Big Earl's guy in the Hood. He had 20-30 students at West who were regular customers, and was putting about $400 a week into his pocket. But with Big Earl dead, and the schools closed, he didn't know what the hell was going on.

Dwight called Damian after Earl's death and was assured it would be business as usual, as Heem Jones and Earl's cousin Sheila were continuing the business. He had no idea who this Jason Rogers was, but Rogers seemed to know him and had his phone number. He could be a student wanting a menu, but he could also be an undercover cop. Dwight planned to play this real cautious-like.

There was an open bench in front of the closed market, and Dwight had himself a seat. Rogers must have been watching the bench as he appeared within seconds and introduced himself as "JRo."

At five foot, nine inches, with dreadlocks, and a creamy mocha complexion, Rogers had on shades, a 76ers warm-up jacket, jeans with holes in both knees, and Nike sneakers.

"Glad to make your acquaintance, Dwight. I understand we are in the same business."

"Oh yeah, and what business would that be?"

"I ain't here to play games, Dwight. My business has been concentrated elsewhere, but I am moving to West Philly, and I understand you have a nice following. With Big Earl gone, you don't know what might happen with his business. I can make this financially attractive to you."

"Damian Mitchell ain't gonna like it."

"Let me worry about Mitchell. You gotta couple of days to decide, Dwight, but I'm talking to other dudes and we need to move. You'd be doing what you're doing, same customers, the same products, and for more money. I'm trying to make this decision easy for you, bruh. Talk soon," Rogers said as he stood and offered his fist to Bridges who bumped it.

Chapter 26

April 14, 2020

Brenda Porter and her teenage daughter, Tawana, lived in a rented house at 57th and Gainor Road in the Wynnefield section of West Philadelphia. With school closed, Tawana was not allowed out and spent all day texting her equally bored friends and watching TV. She never thought she'd miss not going to school, but with everything closed and being unable to hang with friends, returning to school seemed great.

Tawana was five foot, three inches, slender with jet-black hair and a mole over her left brow. Her hair was always in a ponytail or braids. She was athletic and ran a leg of the 1600 meters relay team.

Her mother was a single mom, five foot five inches with the same black hair as her daughter but more full-figured. She got pregnant two years after graduating high school, and divorced two years after that, but she was determined to give her daughter a good life, and education. So far, she thought she was doing OK.

She worked an 8:00-4:00 shift at The Hospital at the University of Pennsylvania as a Phlebotomist in the Outpatient Lab, mostly drawing blood from patients and coordinating pick-up and deliveries with LabCorp. With the COVID outbreak, she was adding testing to her resume. The lines of people for testing grew larger every day and the medical experts on TV were predicting it would get worse. She got home typically around 4:45, but today she was targeting 6:30.

Tawana was scared shitless, and that was an understatement. Tawana had been a "good girl," got decent grades, chose her friends wisely, and, except for trying marijuana two years ago, had avoided high school drug temptations. Until two weeks ago! At a party before COVID made everyone stay home, she and a girlfriend succumbed to peer pressure and tried some new drug everyone had been raving about.

She took an injection in her left arm, and, as promised, it gave her a quick high and a total chill out. She slept at her friend's, and by the time she went home, she was feeling fine. Four days later, she still had some redness, and her arm was itchy. Now, two weeks later, the sore was worsening, oozing, and totally disgusting. She could not avoid telling her mom; she would know what to do.

Brenda Porter got home at 6:45. Tawana was up in her room, texting a friend. She ran downstairs, and before her mom had her coat off, she said, "Mom, I need you to look at this and tell me what I should do." She rolled up her sleeve.

She took her daughter's arm, and leaned in to within two inches to inspect it, "What the hell is that?"

"I don't know, Mom. What should I do?" Tawana hated lying to her mom, but she was too scared to tell her the truth.

"Get your jacket and get in the car. We're running over to the Urgent Care. Let's go!"

The Tower Health Urgent Care was a mile away. They did not always have a doctor there but always had several RNs or PAs. For now, they would do. Brenda and Tawana arrived in less than ten minutes before Brenda had time to interrogate her daughter. She was relieved to have only one person in front of them. They just made it before the 7:00 closing time. Since Tawana had been there before, they only needed to sign in and supply their insurance cards.

While waiting, Brenda finally asked, "Where did you get this, and how long ago?"

"About two weeks ago. Is how really important?"

"You don't think the doctor will ask?"

Before Tawana could answer, the nurse assistant asked them to follow her back to the exam room. She took Tawana's blood pressure and temperature, and reviewed her health history. "What brings you in today?"

Tawana rolled up her sleeve and showed a soreness.

"Oh my, how long have you had that?" The nurse put on gloves and started pressing around the wound.

"Two weeks now. At first, it was just red and a little sore, but it's gotten worse."

"Does it hurt when I touch it?"

Tawana replied, "Not much."

"Have you been bitten or stung by anything?"

"Nope! Not that I am aware of." Tawana couldn't look at the nurse or her mom as she kept withholding the truth. She stammered when she spoke, and her eyes were moist.

"Doctor Carlos Ramsey will be right in."

And he was, carrying Tawana's chart. The boyish-looking doctor had pale skin and short, reddish-blond hair. He was so young that Ms. Porter thought he could have been a classmate of Tawana's. He was wearing a mask and a white coat. As he sat on the stool and rolled up to Tawana, he asked, "Do you mind if I take the mask off? It's easier to talk, and hopefully be understood."

"Absolutely," Tawana's mom answered.

"OK, let's see this sore."

Tawana showed him.

"Do you want to tell me anything, Tawana? Like where you got this?" The doctor's eyebrows raised, inquisitively.

"Mom, do you want to give us some privacy?" She looked pleadingly at her mom.

"Not a chance, Tawana. Tell the doctor," crossing her arms and curling her lip.

Knowing she could no longer avoid a full confession, Tawana bowed her head and asked for a tissue to dry her tears. "OK, first, you need to know that I am not a druggie," Tawana stammered and paused, searching for strength before bursting, "but at a party two weeks ago, I tried this drug everyone was raving about. It gave me a quick, nice high. I wasn't concerned until it started to feel sore and got ugly."

"Oh God, Tawana," her mom interrupted. "How often have we discussed this; taking stuff you don't know what it is or where it came from?"

The doctor spoke, not allowing time for Tawana to say, "Everyone else was doing it'. "I will clean this up and give you an injection of Naloxone. I will call in a prescription for more in the form of a nasal spray. But you need to see an infectious disease doctor immediately." Turning to Brenda, "There are a couple of good ones where you work at HUP, Ms. Porter. I'll give you their names." Turning back to Tawana, he said, "Tawana, have any of your friends mentioned any similar sores?"

"No, not really, but I haven't seen any of them since school closed."

"Ms. Porter, I suggest you contact someone at Overbrook and advise them, and any of the parents of Tawana's friends. I must report this to the police. I don't have to give them your name, just the details. I'd like to speak with you privately, Ms. Porter."

He finished treating Tawana and then showed her back to the waiting room. He came back to Ms. Porter.

"This is potentially serious. The drug that causes this is most likely Xylazine, known on the street as Tranq. It was probably mixed with fentanyl. The medication I injected is Naloxone, which is effective against fentanyl, but, regrettably, not as effective against Tranq. We can only hope that the mix had a small percentage of Tranq, and that is why you need to see a specialist tomorrow, if possible. Sorry, I cannot do more."

This conversation and disclosure left Brenda Porter unsettled, scared, and overwhelmed. She did all she could to hold in her tears and, with difficulty, mumbled, "Thank you, Doctor. We will see someone at HUP tomorrow, as she stood and went to retrieve her daughter.

The ride home was quiet. No one wanted to give or listen to any lecture. There would be time for that later.

Chapter 27

March 12, 2022

James called the office at Overbrook to contact Winston Armstrong, the Security Guard for the last 30 years. The office gave the message to Armstrong, and he returned James's call later that day. Being Bo Campbell's grandfather apparently had some pull.

Armstrong was a beat patrolman for the Philly PD until 1992 when he was shot in a burglary gone bad. Patrol officers were not routinely wearing protective vests in those days, and the gunshot was close to being fatal. It ended Armstrong's days on the beat, and when he was offered the position at Overbrook, he took that over a precinct desk job. The city placed at least one guard in every high school, hoping their mere presence might be enough to keep the kids in order and trouble at bay.

Armstrong quickly got the nickname Quick Draw, even though, in those days, he only carried a club. Five years ago, after updating his handgun qualifications, he started carrying a Standard G19 Glock. He hoped this would be a deterrent to any outside intruders; so far, it had worked. And at six foot four, 260 pounds, Armstrong had a huge physical presence.

He was eligible for retirement, but he relished his work. He found that the very large majority of kids wanted a safe environment at school, and he enjoyed his interaction with many of them. He had to break up the occasional fight and was always on the lookout for weapons and drugs.

Promptly at 2:00, Armstrong met James McNeil at the high school office. They were able to use a small conference room. James noticed Armstrong walked with a slight limp, but he didn't know if it was from the shooting years ago or the size of the man.

Stroking his week-old facial hair, James started, "Thanks, Officer, for making some time for me. I'll try not to keep you too long."

"Glad to make your acquaintance, Mr. McNeil. How's Bo doing? No one here believes he did this."

"Thanks. I appreciate you saying that. Please call me James, and Bo is doing OK, under the circumstances. We are all trying to help his attorney prove Bo's innocence. This cocaine that was planted in Bo's locker would suggest there could be a drug overtone to this murder. What do you know about the drug scene on campus here?"

"Not as much as you might think, James. We know many of the kids are partaking in the various drugs available on the street, but we only catch the occasional transaction here at school. It is my understanding that most exchanges are done off the school grounds."

"I was given the names Spooky Little and Spanky Waters. You know them?"

"On my radar with another couple of kids, but as I said, they play it pretty straight in school."

"Who has access to the kids' lockers?"

"That's part of the mystery. Only a few staff people, Mr. Phelps and Mr. Washington for sure, and a couple of others. I don't even have access. But these locks were not built for Fort Knox, James. I suspect it would not take Jesse James to break into one."

"Have you been interviewed yet by the detectives handling the case?"

"I have. Roberta Rumson was in the other day. I told her pretty much what I told you."

"That's most of my questions, Winston. I do appreciate your time and willingness to speak with me."

"Anything I can do to help Bo, I'm glad to do, James. Here, take my cell number should anything come up," writing the number on a notepad and handing it to James.

"Thanks again."

James was not sure he had made any progress. He got no names that he didn't already have from Carl Watkins. And these kids were all at Overbrook; Sherman Claxton was a student at Widener, even though any drug connections might go back to West Philly High. James understood that Overbrook and West Philly were so close that it was likely the same person was working both schools. Little and Waters were low-level runners and would not have the motive to kill Claxton or frame Bo. No, this would have had to come from the top, and since Big Earl was murdered two years ago, it was unclear who was on top. He would ask Kenny Anderson to contact Brahim Jones, Earl's #2 guy, and presumably still handling Earl's business.

Kenny Anderson had been James's father, Lincoln McNeil's, best friend for about sixty years since they were both sophomores at West Philly High School and tried to date Shirley Williams at the same time. Shirley could not stand either one of them.

They had gone in the Army together but got split up after Basic Training, with Anderson going to Viet Nam and McNeil to Korea. After the service, they both used the GI Bill to attend Philadelphia College of Textiles and Sciences; Anderson graduated with a Business Admin degree, but McNeil had moved on to the Curtis School of Music.

They never lived more than five blocks from each other and were the Godfathers of each other's kids, including James. Bo's brother was named after him.

But on the streets of West Philly, Kenny Anderson was simply *THE MAN.* He spent the last twenty-five years walking the streets, talking to everyone who might listen, some who would not. If something went down in West Philly, Anderson knew who, what and why. He was often contacted by the local police for information but he was discreet about dropping the dime on his local brothers.

James placed a call to Anderson's cell, and he answered on the first ring.

"Hey James, what's going on?"

"Samo, samo Godfather, and you?"

"Ditto. How's Bo doing?"

"OK, I guess, but that's why I am calling. How much do you know?"

"Assume nothing, and you won't be too far off."

"OK, you know Sherman went to West Philly, but drugs were found in Bo's locker. We are assuming there is a drug connection to the murder. We have a couple of names of kids running at Overbrook but don't know who's supplying these kids. They could have been Big Earl's kids. I was hoping you might contact Heem Jones and find out who his runners are at Overbrook and who might be the players at West Philly."

"Give me the kids' names, James. It would be easier for Heem to confirm names that I have rather than give me the names of kids I don't have."

"Makes sense, Kenny. The names I've got so far are Spooky Little and Spanky Waters."

"Give me a day or two. I'll get back to you. Is Bo's sister, Claudia, defending him?"

"She's helping, but we have a heavyweight named Fred Chasnoff."

"I know the name. Give Bo and his family my best, James. We'll talk again soon."

Chapter 28

April 14, 2020

Dwight Bridges had texted Jason Rogers that he was in, willing to start working with him at once at West Philly when school reopened. They would get together soon to discuss the details. As Dwight figured, the kids would not know that he was doing anything different. All they knew was that he was their contact and the amount they were paying for their order.

But Bridges knew he could not play both sides for long. Damian Mitchell would soon notice that his revenue was off, and JRo would not see as much revenue as he expected. If only he could add new customers but that also would have to wait until school resumed. That would delay his day of reckoning. But what was Mitchell to do? And JRo said he would handle Mitchell, right?

And he was only in this until graduation in June. He'd stay clean at Philly Community College.

Tawana and her mother were at the Hospital of the University of Pennsylvania. Using her contacts there at HUP, Brenda Porter secured an appointment with Dr. Thomas Albright, Chief of Infectious Diseases at HUP. They had already taken Tawana's blood and been interviewed by the PA. They now anxiously awaited Dr. Albright.

He entered the room with a smile and introduced himself. He was tall, lean, clean shaven, and in scrubs. He was carrying and still glancing at Tawana's file. Nothing he could do though would alleviate the anxiety of mother or daughter.

"Let's take a look at this arm." He closed the file, placed it on the desk, and pulled over a stool.

Tawana pulled up her sleeve and held it out for Albright's inspection.

"It appears this fellow at the Urgent Care did the right thing. Had you delayed seeing someone another day or two, well, there is no sense speculating. This is a fentanyl infection and is serious. We'll get the blood results, and that should let us know just how serious. We are seeing a few of these cases, and the outcomes vary widely. I don't wish to scare you, but then again, maybe I should. We have seen deaths and amputations, but also full recoveries. The variables seem to be the mix of this Tranq and fentanyl and the time before treatment. Kids have the wrong idea that if they are not addicted, they are safe, but we see as many one-time users here as we do addicts."

"When will we know for sure, Doctor?" Brenda Porter asked.

"We will know when we get the blood results, the approximate mix of drugs, but continue the meds your Urgent Care doctor prescribed. If the sore gets any worse, call the office here. The next two-to-three days will tell the story. Let's hope for the best and that this turns out to be only a very dangerous and scary lesson."

"Thank you, Doctor. We'll be in touch."

Chapter 29

March 15, 2022

After graduating from Villanova Law School, Claudia Campbell joined a small Mom & Pop law firm in Ardmore. Patty Larsen was a good friend of Claudia's mom, and she and her husband Jim had a boutique law firm with more work than either could manage. They were glad to bring Claudia into the firm.

A general practice, they dealt with real estate transactions, Wills and Trusts, domestic issues including divorces, civil actions, and misdemeanors.

Claudia finished her 3:00 client meeting at 4:20. She was relieved to find only one voicemail message, from an unknown phone number. She listened to the message, "Hello, Claudia? This is Melanie Wexler from Fred Chasnoff's office. I'll be in the Bala Cynwyd area at about 6:00 and wondered if you might be available for a drink. It would be a chance to get acquainted. Let me know either way, call or text. Thanks."

What's that about? Claudia wondered. *Something up on the case?* But she had nothing on her calendar and thought networking was always a good thing. She texted, "Sounds good! How about the lounge at the City Ave? 6:00?"

Even at rush hour, it would only take fifteen minutes to get to the Hilton, allowing Claudia time to clean up some paperwork. Patty and Jim were still in the office when she said goodnight at 5:40.

She pulled up to the valet at 5:55 and walked into the lounge. There were six people at the small bar, and she saw Melanie waving from a small table at the rear of the lounge. There were only two other tables occupied; this was always a quiet place unless there was a business meeting going on at the hotel. Apparently, there was none today.

Melanie stood as Claudia reached the table, offered her hand, and said, "Welcome! Glad the timing worked."

"Me too. Thanks for the invite. You live out this way?"

"No, I live at The View at 4th and Race Street, but I had a meeting in our Bala office, so I thought I might wait until rush hour was over before heading back into the city. How about you?"

"I live at The Yard, the new apartments down by the river in Bala. A big move for me out of West Philly. Are you a Philly girl?"

"Maybe now, but I'm from the Hartford area, actually Bristol, but came down here for undergrad at Haverford, then Penn Law, and been here since then. Where did you go to school?"

"St. Joe's undergrad, then Villanova Law. Looks like I'll never get out of the city."

"Hey, you're in Bala now, that's stepping out. So, how are Bo and the family holding up by now?"

"All things considered, I guess, OK. But we all wonder just how this could happen. My brother is a good, clean kid."

"We'll figure it out. I still believe in the end, justice prevails. So, what is your personal life like?"

"Nothing terribly exciting. I ran track in high school and college, and still like to run for a loop down by the river. Next year I hope to do *The Broad Street Run*. I try to read a book a week. On Saturdays, I volunteer at the Youth Center in West Philly. That keeps me connected to my roots. Thursday afternoon I work with a group of junior and senior girls at Overbrook who have named themselves *NOCEILING4US*. We discuss potential careers, the need to have and be role models, college plans, you name it. I love these girls."

"Wow! Nice going, girl. You haven't mentioned any guys. You dating anyone special?"

"Not really! I date on occasion but nothing too serious yet. With work, running, volunteering, and family, my life is good right now. How about you? You're so totally gorgeous, there must be a guy in your life."

"About the same as you Claudia, I date occasionally but nothing serious. I had a heavy two-year relationship in college but not heavy enough to sustain after graduation. Work keeps me busy, and I work with a group of future lawyers out at Swarthmore."

By this time, they had had a second drink and some cheesesteak egg rolls. Melanie looked at her watch, and said, "Wow, it's 7:30 already, I didn't mean to take up your entire night. I think it's safe to venture out to the Expressway by now."

"This has been fun, Melanie, thanks for suggesting it. I'll get the attention of the server for a bill."

"Taken care of, Claudia. You can get it next time. Perhaps you'll come into the city, and we can have dinner?"

"That was sneaky of you, but thanks. And I will do it next time, and as much as I hate to drive into the city, I can handle it once or twice a year. You're on!"

They walked out to the valet station and gave them their parking tickets. Melanie's fire-engine red Mini Cooper arrived first. They hugged, and off she went. Claudia's white RAV4 arrived two minutes later. Claudia drove off thinking this was a nice night, and Melanie seemed sweet for such a beautiful, intelligent, high-energy type woman.

Chapter 30

May 10, 2020

Myron Rosen and his wife, Cindy had gotten the kids off to bed at 9:15. The house was quiet as they sat in the family room; Cindy with a book and Myron with his laptop, reviewing his lesson plans for tomorrow.

But the silence did not last long. Myron said, "Cindy, I can't hold off Swarthmore any longer. With school closed, they were good enough to give me another two weeks. We need to decide tonight."

"I know, Hon. I'm sorry for procrastinating but this is such a huge decision for the family. Our life seems so good right now and I know we would not have to move, but your life will be even busier than it is now. And even at Swarthmore, there will be pressure to win, you know that, right?"

"Cind, there is pressure to win wherever I coach. It's part of the job description. We've been fortunate at Overbrook, but I don't know where the next Bo Campbell will come from. We could take a downturn and who knows how long we can continue winning."

"You don't think Luther would fire you if you had a couple of down seasons, do you? And let's not minimize your coaching ability. That has greatly contributed to your success."

"Friendship only goes so far. And great players will beat great coaching every day."

"Look, Ron, I don't want to hold you back from your dreams, so I'll support your decision. There, the decision is all yours. Wasn't that easy?"

"Good! I want to stay at Overbrook, at least another couple of years. We have a solid chance to do something special, and I don't want to let down the kids. If I was more comfortable with a successor, I'd feel different. We've discussed Mac, and I just don't think he's the right guy. I'll call Luther right now and Swarthmore in the morning."

"You could have made this so much easier and quicker had you told me this three weeks ago."

Myron stood up, kissed Cindy, and went to the kitchen to make his call.

At 7:30 the next morning, Overbrook Principal Clarence Phelps, Vice Principal Luther Washington, and Security Guard Winston Armstrong were at their computers conducting a Zoom conference. They exchanged pleasantries, waiting for the serious talk to begin. Washington and Armstrong were waiting on Phelps; he had called the meeting and they expected it to be important, most likely about COVID.

Phelps began, "Thanks guys for the early morning call. As you know, in the three weeks since Tawana Walker contracted her fentanyl infection, we have had two more cases. Ron Walker is still hospitalized and, if he lives, most likely will lose his arm. I called the Superintendent and she is obviously concerned. Our school is not the only one experiencing this and the Super thinks we need some district-wide plan of attack. School being closed may be a good thing for a while, but we still have a responsibility here. You have any thoughts?"

Armstrong spoke first, "We have discussed this before, but we believe that most of this activity is happening outside of school. It seems the best we can do is educate and warn the kids and their parents of the dangers."

"Luther?" Phelps asked.

"I know we try to respect the privacy of the students, but we could resume making locker inspections. Even though they may be buying these drugs outside of school, I have to believe many of them are keeping them in their lockers rather than their bedrooms."

Phelps added, "I think these kids discuss with each other the cool high they get from these drugs, and when they hear someone got sick or died, they think that was a junkie. Not so. We are hearing that so many were first-time, or infrequent users. Win, have you had any contact with the local police?"

"I did speak with Captain Webster at the 55th Precinct. She said when school resumed, she would ask her team to have a greater presence between 2:30 and 4:30 when school is dismissed, but she also added that these kids aren't stupid. They are very cautious."

"Let's try this: first we'll conduct an assembly this week via Zoom. I'll tell them about these most recent situations, read them the Riot Act, and tell them we intend to enforce a zero-tolerance policy for possession, selling, or using any illegal drug in school or on the grounds.

Secondly, I'll send an email to all the parents and follow that up with a written copy making certain they are all aware of the seriousness of this matter.

Lastly, with school closed, I don't think there is any sense in conducting locker inspections. We can defer that decision until school resumes, if it does, this semester."

Phelps concluded, "I'll get back to you on the timing of all of this. I appreciate your input and support. I think it is critical that we do our very best to nip this in the bud. I'm not naïve that we will stop all drug use, but we must do our best to deliver this message. Thanks, guys."

Chapter 31

March 19, 2022

Kenny Anderson and James McNeil had agreed to meet at Dunkin' at 10:30 in between the morning and lunch traffic.

After they both had their coffees and found a quiet table, James asked, "OK Godfather, whatcha got?"

"I spoke with Heem Jones. He says that since Big Earl's death, the competition has increased in West Philly and now he has at least two other drug teams in his market. One is not a shock, Pops Williams, Earl's old nemesis from Southwest. Earl knew Pops was sniffing around West Philly when he was alive. The third team is a mystery. Heem says a guy that goes by JRo seems to be running it, but Heem doubts this kid is the brains. They started at West Philly High, but now have runners at Overbrook, St. Joe's, and West Catholic High. Heem says they lost 40% of their business and this market cannot support three teams."

"That's a shame Kenny, poor Heem," James said sarcastically. "Did you ask him about how any of this might tie in to Claxton's murder, and Bo's frame-up?"

"I did, and he assured me his team was not involved in any way, but he does believe that one of the other teams is most likely involved. He is guessing that Claxton learned something he was not supposed to and may have shared it with Bo. Killing Claxton and framing Bo would eliminate them both."

"But if Bo knew anything, he would have shared it with someone by now. I'll tell Claudia and let her run with it."

The girl behind the counter approached their table holding a coffee pot and carrying two chocolate-covered donuts with rainbow jimmies. "More coffee, gentlemen?"

Kenny asked, "Dunkin' providing table service now, Brittney?"

"Only for special customers, Mr. Anderson." They both accepted the coffee and donuts and thanked her.

In between bites and sips, they got caught up on their respective families and, by noon, they had gone their separate ways.

James called and updated Claudia on what he had learned from Kenny. It gave Claudia an excuse to call Melanie, whom she had not heard from since their drinks the other night. "Hey girl, what's going on?"

"Am I catching you at a good time, Mel?"

"Absolutely, just reading depositions. You will keep me awake. What's up?"

"I don't think you've met my grandfather yet, James McNeil. Since he helped Detective Brown catch his father's murderer two years ago, he's been playing amateur sleuth. Anyway, he and his Godfather have learned from a source that there is speculation that Sherman Claxton had found out something he should not have, and he was eliminated, and had Bo framed, to protect that secret."

"Any idea who the bad guys might be?"

"There seem to be three competing drug teams in the West Philly area, and they are not exactly friendly competitors. There is a belief that one of the groups has a behind-the-scenes boss, and that could be the tie in. Have you guys come up with anything?"

"Our investigator, Tyrone Hill, spoke with Sherman's parents who were shocked and in denial that he might have been involved with drugs in any way. He then spoke with several of his old teammates and coach at West Philly and two teammates at Widener. The kids at West said they were aware that Sherman had experimented with Oxy, but both believed he was not a regular user. The coach knew nothing, nor did his teammates at Widener. We think that Sherman's drug use was not an issue, nor was he in debt. Your theory that he may have learned something makes more sense. I'll update Fred. Thanks, Claudia. And when are you coming into town and paying off that dinner debt?"

"I knew you wouldn't forget that. I'm busy this weekend but how about a week from Saturday? You pick the place."

"Works for me. It will cost you. Talk later!"

Was she really becoming a friend to Melanie? Claudia thought to herself as she hung up.

Chapter 32

May 12, 2020

Two days after he met with Armstrong and Washington, Principal Phelps went live on Zoom.

Students, first, I hope that you and your families are all safe and taking every precaution the CDC has recommended against COVID-19. This is a serious disease and don't be fooled thinking that because you are young and healthy, this cannot hit you. We hope to know more about if or when school might resume, or if conducting Zoom classes is possible.

But I want to address another serious situation today. That is drug use. I know you all believe you have heard this before, and that you are all smarter than your parents and our team here at Overbrook.

In the last two months, we have had ten cases of fentanyl infections. One of your classmates is still at the University of Pennsylvania Hospital and the doctors are not certain he will live. On the street, this drug is known as Tranq, as well as other names, and is a hybrid of fentanyl cut with the animal tranquilizer xylazine. As we understand it, the more xylazine in the mix, the more dangerous it becomes, and there is no way to know what the mix is until it is too late.

We want you to know that nine of these ten affected students were not regular drug users, but simply decided to try it with friends. If you think by only trying it once, you will be safe, you would be wrong.

We, of course, do not encourage the use of any illegal recreational drugs but are making this Tranq situation enemy number one.

We also know that you are buying these drugs from fellow students. I am telling those students that they are potentially killing their friends and classmates for a couple of bucks. Please think about that.

Any student caught using, selling, or possessing any illegal drugs will be expelled from school and reported to the local police.

With the summer break approaching, we hope you will make good decisions, and be back with us in September.

The call ended. No one could be certain of the impact on the students. Time would tell!

Chapter 33

May 13, 2020

By the time Assistant Coach Reggie McIntosh had learned that Coach Rosen had been offered the coaching job at Swarthmore College, he also learned that he had declined it, and would be remaining at Overbrook. It appeared that Big Mac would remain an assistant for the foreseeable future. Perhaps it was time to look for a head coaching position at another school. Due to his other business interests, he preferred to remain in the West Philadelphia area. There were other schools but turnover at these coaching positions was not frequent. Perhaps he should give up coaching entirely. He taught Physical Education and, if he gave up coaching, he'd have more time to focus on other activities.

He would give this considerable thought over the summer.

Chapter 34

June 10, 2020

Coach Rosen had to conduct his annual pre-summer message via Zoom to his team. Since their annual postseason dinner in March, they had not been together as a unit, and he wanted to reconnect before the summer.

OK, guys! No long speech today but I did want to get us all together, if you can call Zoom a get-together, for one last time before our summer break.

First, I want to congratulate and thank you graduating seniors, Carl, Ron, Larry, and Julio. We'll miss you guys, and we wish you the very best. Come back and visit, you hear?

The rest of you work on your games. See me if you want to discuss which part of your game needs improvement, otherwise, assume your entire game needs it. If you are playing in any summer league, please limit it to one. You hear that, Bo? Not Narberth, Tustin and Haddington, just one! It might help if you played together. You know I cannot be involved as the rules say we cannot practice as a team in the summer. I wish I could tell you that these leagues will be playing this summer, but if not, so be it.

More than anything, y'all need to make good decisions this summer. Have fun, but as I used to tell my sister, have a sensible good time. Stay away from drugs, alcohol, and trouble. You heard the principal. There is zero tolerance for violations.

Have a great summer, guys. Meeting adjourned.

Bo would be a junior next season, the expectations would be high, and anything less than city and state championships would be disappointing. Bo would not let them down.

Chapter 35

July 10, 2020

The balance of the school semester had been canceled, and there would be no summer basketball, or anything else. Schools were preparing for Zoom classes in September.

Ron Walker had died in the hospital of complications from the fentanyl infection. Six new cases had been reported and we were losing the war on drugs.

But the big story throughout the world was COVID-19. It had become clear that the politicians had downplayed the seriousness of this disease, adding to its spread. It was going to be a hot topic in the Presidential election in November, perhaps the only topic. Deaths and hospitalizations were increasing every day. The health care resources all over the world were overloaded.

Even the drug world could not escape the wrath of COVID. Rahim, Pops, and Mr. B had all picked a bad time to expand. With most of their customers home on forced or voluntary quarantine, no one had figured out how to continue distribution. COVID was doing to the drug business what no government PSA's ever could; slowly killing their business.

All and all, it was a real shitshow, as the kids liked to say.

Bo's only outlets were his five to ten mile a day runs and practicing his foul and three-point shooting over at Tustin. Alone! Carl was allowed to join him today after both their parents lectured about masks, social distancing, blah, blah. *How you supposed to practice social distancing and play defense at the same time*, Bo wondered.

They met at 10:00 hoping to beat the mid-afternoon heat. They didn't; it was already 87 degrees and with 84% humidity. This would not be a fun workout. A thunderstorm would be a welcome reprieve.

They played one-on-one for about an hour and then played H-O-R-S-E for another forty-five minutes before calling it quits. Catching their breath while gulping water, Carl asked Bo, "You hear about Ron Walker?"

"Yeah, that's fucked-up. You know him?"

"He was in my algebra class. I didn't know him really well, but he seemed like a nice kid. It's all horrible."

"Tawana Porter had a bad case of it, but I heard she's better now. What's going on with these kids, Carl?"

"I don't know." Bo shrugged. "You got any plans for the rest of the week?"

"Not really. You?" Carl asked Bo.

"Thursday I'm going down to Haddington to practice with Sherm. Wanna come?"

"Thanks, I'll pass on that, but we'll do this again Friday or Saturday."

"Maybe Friday AND Saturday. How about a run in the morning? 8:00 good?"

"I'll be there, bruh. Later."

They exchanged fist bumps and took off.

That same morning, Brahim Jones was waiting for Damian Mitchell in the parking lot of ReAnimator Coffee at 47th and Pine Streets in West Philly. The coffee shop was only available for drive-thru business, which he had done, picking up a black coffee and a glazed donut for Mitchell.

At 10:10, Mitchell climbed into the car, and said, "What's going on, Heem? That coffee for me?"

"Yeah, Dame. All good with you?"

"I gotta tell you, Heem, if school don't resume in September, I might have to go out and find a real job." Damian took a huge bite of his donut.

"Tell me about it, bruh. But we got other problems, don't we?"

"If you mean about Dwight, yeah, we do. I contacted a couple of his regular customers and they said they were still getting their stuff from Dwight, meaning Dwight ain't getting his stuff from us. I think he's getting it from a guy named JRo, but I don't know the dude."

"That jives with what Spanky told me. He said a new kid named Garrett Green was working the Overbrook kids, and this JRo was his supplier."

"Got a plan, Heem?"

"I told Sheila after Earl died that I was hoping to avoid violence, but I don't see how I can. Either Dwight or this JRo needs to go, Dame. What do you think?"

"I agree, Heem. And since this JRo is hurting us in multiple places, he'd be my choice."

"Why don't you keep your eye on Dwight, try to find out who this JRo is, and where he hangs? I'll ask Spanky to do the same with this Green kid. Once we ID this guy, we'll formulate our plan. Meanwhile, stay safe and keep your kids calling their customers. We need the business."

"Don't I know that Heem. Stay safe yourself."

Chapter 36

March 23, 2022

Detective Vernon Brown was in his cubicle at the 55th Street HQ building, when the Desk Sergeant on Duty, Wilson Hightower, buzzed him. "Whaddaya got, Wil?" Brown asked.

"I have a woman down here with her son. She'd like to talk to the Detective handling the Bo Campbell case. Says her son went to West Philly when Sherman Claxton was there and has something you ought to know."

"Can you put her in a conference room, Wil? I'll be down in just a couple."

"Will do, Vern."

Vern wondered what his might be. Clues and witnesses had been scarce, and he was getting a lot of pressure from the DA's office because he needed something concrete. It was one thing to hope that Bo was innocent, but it was his job to prove he was guilty. *This kid might have got something that could move the needle in one direction*? he asked himself.

He walked into the conference room, and introduced himself, "Good morning. I am Detective Brown. May I ask your names?"

"Yes, Detective. I am Myah Weeks, and this is my son, Deforia. Deforia, you need to tell the detective what you know." She nudged her son gently toward Brown.

"Thank you both for coming in. What can you tell me, son?"

Deforia was dressed in drooping baggy jeans, an Eagles sweatshirt, and a 76ers cap. It seemed obvious to Brown the kid did not want to be here; his mom must have insisted he do the right thing. He was fidgeting, looking around the room, anything but looking Brown in the eye.

"Will I have to be a witness at the trial, sir?"

"I can't answer that right now. That will be up to the District Attorney."

"I don't know that this has anything to do with Sherman's murder, but he and Bo Campbell were an item."

"What do you mean, an *item*?"

"You know, hooking up. They were gay."

"Wait, let's back up. How do you know Claxton?"

"We were teammates at West Philly. Sherman was a year ahead of me. He graduated two years ago, and I graduated last June."

"OK, so again, what, when, and where did you see whatever you saw?"

"It was about a year ago. I work part-time down at *Beiler's Donuts in the Reading Terminal Market.* I look up and see these two walking with their arms around each other."

"Could they have been fooling around?"

"Sir, if that's what you wanna believe, go for it, but I know what I saw, and that was no fooling around."

"Have you told anyone else about this?" Brown asked.

"Nah, I really didn't think much about it, but when Sherm got killed, I thought I should tell my mom."

"That's fine! I'll have you wait in the lobby while I have your statement typed up, then you may go. I'll be back in touch if we need anything else. I appreciate your both coming in. You did the right thing, Deforia."

They all stood, and Brown escorted them back to the lobby, where he said farewell.

Walking back to his cubicle, Brown thought, *This doesn't make Bo the murderer, but it gives the DA a possible motive. I wonder what James knows.*

Later, having dinner that night with his wife Ronnie, Vernon asked, "Are there times you ever hate your job, Ron?"

"Me? Only a half dozen times a day or so. What's up?" Ronnie was a pediatric nurse at the Children's Hospital of Pennsylvania, better known as CHOP to Philadelphians.

Vern told her about Deforia Weeks' story, adding, "I know in my heart that Bo didn't do this, but this gives evidence to the DA. James will shit!"

Placing her loving hand on his, Ronnie said, "Look Vern, all you can do is your job, and that is, search for the truth. And if you find it, perhaps that will exonerate Bo. I know you do not want to consider the alternative, but that is a possibility too."

"I don't even want to go there, but thanks for the reminder."

Chapter 37

August 12, 2020

Things were quiet on the streets of West Philadelphia. The Summer of COVID was proving to be a dreadful summer for the drug business as well as restaurants and all other respectable retail businesses. The news said that golf courses were benefiting as people could be outside and social distance. And runners, walkers, and birders loved to be alone.

It was a typical August day, hot and humid, even at 9:00 in the morning.

Damian Mitchell was parked a half block away from Dwight Bridges' house in the 6100 block of Jefferson Street in West Philadelphia. Close enough to see the front door, but far enough away not to be noticed. He could only do this a day or two a week, but it seemed better than only periodically circling the ghost town of the Overbrook High campus.

Damian was not the most patient person and, by 10:30, he was about ready to call it a day. But he caught a break. Dwight came out of his house and walked toward 60th Street, in the opposite direction from Dwight. He knew he had to follow Dwight on foot, so he exited the car, locked it, and followed Dwight, staying a comfortable hundred yards behind him.

Dwight made a left on 59th Street, heading toward Overbrook High. As they got closer, it was clear that Dwight was getting in line for water ice. The water ice stand across from Overbrook had been there as long as the school, or at least that was the legend. It had changed owners many times, and Billy King now owned it. His teenage son and daughter were working today, and the line was ten deep. The customers were observing social distancing, and all but two had on a mask.

Philadelphia claimed to be the capital of the water ice world, and Rita's, the not-quite national chain, was opened in 1984 by Bob Tomolo and named after his wife. King's Water Ice was one of many that saturated Philadelphia.

Within fifteen minutes, Dwight had his water ice and walked toward a car parked thirty yards toward Damian, but he was still at a safe distance to observe. The driver got out of his blue 2016 Camry and stood at his trunk waiting for Dwight. Just two brothers sharing a water ice. Damian wished he had one of those telephoto lenses they all had on TV, but the zoom lens of his iPhone would have to do. He got a pretty good shot of Dwight and whom he suspected to be JRo.

This JRo put something in Dwight's backpack; it could have been drugs. Damian considered running back to get his car and follow JRo but thought better of it as Dwight and JRo parted and JRo got back into his car.

He texted the picture to Brahim Jones and walked back to his car hoping that the mystery was solved.

Chapter 38

August 25, 2020

Over the weekend, Sherman and Bo had agreed to meet at Sunny's on 52nd Street, midway between their homes. Sherman was heading back to Widener this coming weekend, and Philadelphia schools were scheduled to re-open after Labor Day. COVID was still a presence, but they felt the risks could be managed, and Zoom teaching was less than ideal.

Bo and Sherman gulped down their burgers, fries, and Cokes with small talk about their upcoming seasons, classes, and the usual. As they exited, Bo said, "We need to talk, Sherm."

"Didn't you once tell me that no one needs to talk?"

"I may have, but we do need to talk."

"I'm listening."

"OK, here goes. I'm attracted to you so I'm thinking I'm gay, and I'm scared shitless about it."

Sherman had hoped this day would come, but now that it was here, he was unsettled. He was more than attracted to Bo, he truly thought he loved this guy. Sherman had a couple of gay hook-ups, but never a relationship.

He put his hand on Bo's shoulder, and said, "Bo, the feeling is mutual, but I'm scared also. And heading back to school, I'm not certain what the next step should be. How about after I get settled, you come down the following Saturday? You can catch the subway down to the Sports Complex, we can meet at Xfinity, and grab something to eat."

Bo had goosebumps but he continued fidgeting; "Can we keep this on the DL?"

"Absolutely! You're still looking for a college, and I believe no one knows about me. Look, Bo, I'm excited about our potential, but I think we need to take this slow and be discreet." Glancing around, Sherm quickly patted Bo's hand, as they both stood.

"Amen, bruh. Gotta run. we'll talk."

They exchanged a brief hug and headed their separate ways. Bo wondered where all this might lead but he knew he could not fight the inevitable.

Chapter 39

March 26, 2022

James McNeil sat in his son's office at PhillyBeats when his cell phone rang; it was Vernon Brown. "Good morning, Vern, what's going on?"

"Not a whole lot, James, but I've got an update you ought to know about."

"You're dropping the case on Bo for lack of evidence?"

"Don't I wish! We had a witness come in who'll testify that Bo and Sherman were in a romantic relationship."

"Old news, Vern, and it sure don't mean he killed Sherman. Makes it more unlikely he did. Why would he kill someone he cared about?"

"The DA will speculate there was a lover's spat or one of them was breaking it off, cheating on the other, whatever."

"I doubt there will be any evidence to that."

"James, my friend, let me tell you how murder trials work. First, you need to understand that the jury wants someone to pay for murdering this twenty-year-old boy. The trial becomes a story, and the DA's story will be that Bo and Sherman were lovers, and they had a falling out. Bo was unable to accept the relationship ending, got a gun, and killed Sherman. Then hid the weapon in his locker until he could dispose of it. All nice and tidy."

"And then Chasnoff will tell our story that Bo would not kill his best friend, Sherman, that there are no witnesses, no fingerprints on the gun, and the evidence was planted. I'm surprised you guys would even bring this to trial, Vernon."

"Off the record, James, that still would be both of our best hopes. Anyway, I wanted you to know what we now know."

"I appreciate that Vern, but we assumed when we learned of the Bo, Claxton relationship, that you would hear about it and use it. Hey, can we get the girls together and go out for dinner, or do we need for this case to be done?"

"No, that's a good idea, James. I'll mention it to Ronnie and have her coordinate it with Linda. See you soon, James."

Chapter 40

May 30, 2022

Philadelphia had long had a vibrant and diverse dining scene, from the nationally famed Zahav to the neighborhood bar/restaurant like Stogie Joe's. More recently, Vietnamese, Mexican, and Pakistani cuisines had been added to the long-established Italian, Steak, and Seafood. New ones always come and go, but in Philadelphia, like her residents, only the strong survived.

Melanie had chosen one of those survivors for tonight's dinner with Claudia. *The Saloon* in the 700 block of South 7th Street in the heart of South Philadelphia was opened in 1967. Very few restaurants could claim Best Italian and Best Steakhouse, but *The Saloon* could. And no need to advertise; if you didn't know about The Saloon, they were always fully booked with those that did.

For reasons she could not fully comprehend, Claudia spent an inordinate amount of time selecting her outfit and jewelry before settling on a Kelly-green dress, gold and jade bangle bracelets, and pendant. She thought she looked pretty good.

Claudia could think of nothing worse than driving into Philadelphia on a Saturday night, but she would get creative and avoid Center City by taking West River Drive, jumping onto the Schuylkill Expressway at the Art Museum, and exiting onto Passyunk Avenue, up to 7th Street. Leaving herself plenty of time for their 7:00 PM reservation, she arrived at 6:50.

The Saloon actually had a parking lot, but it only held about ten cars, so she left it with the valet. She wondered just where the valet took the cars since there was never any place in South Philly to park. Probably better she did not know.

She walked into the small, crowded bar area and was greeted by an attractive hostess. Melanie had beaten her here, and she was led to a table in the rear.

Melanie stood to greet her, and they exchanged hugs. This dining room was a small one with only six tables, so the noise level was reasonable compared to most restaurants these days. It was tastefully furnished and decorated with pictures of Italy and Philadelphia.

As she sat and got settled, Claudia asked, "How did you find this place?"

"I was here a couple of years ago celebrating the acquittal of one of our clients. I said then I'd be back, but I usually wind up going to restaurants I can walk to. I think you'll like it. It's been here forever, and you cannot go wrong with anything on the menu. How was the drive in?"

"All things considered, not too bad. I used the Expressway into Passyunk. How about you?"

"I Ubered. I hate driving in the city, and parking down here is impossible. And, I can drink."

"I'll have a drink or two myself. I'm thinking wine. You?"

Melanie perused the wine menu. "Not a bad idea. If we can agree on something, we can get a bottle. What is your preference?"

"I'm not real fussy. Something white and dry?"

Not recognizing any of the labels, Melanie suggested an *Australian Sauvignon Blanc*. Claudia gave her approval, and they gave their order to the patiently waiting server, Antonio.

"You look great Claudia. Green is definitely your color."

"You look pretty hot yourself, Mel. This isn't a date, is it?"

Melanie smiled and replied, "Whatever you want it to be, Claudia."

Fortunately, Antonio returned with their wine and an ice bucket that he stood next to the table. He opened the bottle, offered the cork to Melanie, and poured a taste for them both. They approved, he topped their glasses, and asked, "Any questions about the menu? We have two special entrees tonight, Prime Rib served with a horseradish sauce, Hasselback Potatoes and asparagus, and Chilean Sea Bass, in a marinara sauce served over pasta."

"Thank you," Melanie said, "We haven't even looked yet, please give us a few minutes."

"Certainly, take your time."

He left and Claudia made a toast, "To new friends, and good health, and Bo's acquittal." They smiled and clinked glasses. They perused the menu, made their decisions, and settled back.

"Any update on Bo's case?" Claudia asked.

"Strange case, Claudia. It *has* to be about drugs but neither Bo nor Claxton were part of that scene. Our investigator is still trying to identify all the players in both Overbrook and West Philly Highs. He's got about eight, but so far, no connection to Bo or Claxton. You working on anything interesting?"

"Not really, but we are keeping busy with Wills and Trusts, Real Estate, and Domestic cases, so I'm not complaining. I like the small, family atmosphere at the firm."

Noticing the young ladies had put down their menus, Antonio reappeared and asked, "Are we ready to order, ladies?"

They looked at each other and Melanie led the way. "We'll share a Caesar Salad, and I'll have the *Bronzino Grenoblaise*."

Claudia added, "And I'll have the *Linguini Pescatore*."

Antonio refilled their wine glasses and skulked away.

The remainder of the night was much of the same; two professional women enjoying good food and drink, and each other's company. They passed on dessert, Claudia paid her debt and the check, and gave her valet ticket to Antonio. Melanie ordered her Uber.

At the front door, they embraced, and Melanie said, "This was great Claudia, thanks so much. Now we are even, we can go Dutch in the future. Are you sure you are OK to drive?"

"Yep, I'm good, thanks. I enjoyed this immensely. Have a good night."

Chapter 41

October 12, 2020

Jessica and Bo had not seen each other since COVID broke in the spring, even though they continued to text or FaceTime daily. They had never discussed Jessica's attempted kiss or Bo's rejection of the same.

Schools had resumed in September, but things were not back to normal. Masks, social distancing, remote classes, and now they said a vaccine might be available by the end of the year.

"Hey Bo, whatta ya know?" Jessica answered a call from Bo.

"The usual, Jess. Y'all good out there? How about getting together?"

"We are all good, but my parents are total nutjobs about this COVID. They are still wiping down their groceries before bringing them into the house. It would be great to see you. When and where?"

"I'll catch a train at the Overbrook Station. Noon at Not Your Average Joe's in Ardmore? We can figure out where to eat then." Joe's was a high-end burger joint but it was right in the middle of the Ardmore shopping area, and often a meeting spot.

"Sounds good, see you there, Bo."

Ardmore was a tony suburb on Philadelphia's Main Line, five miles west of the City Avenue boundary, and Suburban Square was the toniest section of Ardmore. It included a West Elm, Trader Joe's, Lululemon, Shake Shack, and an Apple Store, with luxury condos and apartments surrounding it.

The train left Bo a five-minute walk from Joe's and when he walked up at 11:50, Jessica was waiting on the bench.

"Yo Bo!" She stood and greeted him. They were both masked-up and there was no usual hug, just a fist bump. "You want to eat?"

"Yeah," Bo replied, "But not here. How about over at the Farmer's Market, pick up a piece of pizza?"

"Good by me." And they walked off. She asked, "How's school for you guys?"

"It's good to be back, but it is so weird. It's like no one knows how to act, what to do, where to sit. I guess everyone seems to be learning about this COVID on the fly. But it's a real shit-show. And we're supposed to start practice on the first, and we still don't know for sure if that'll happen. How about you rich guys?"

Giving him the finger, she said, "The rich guys don't seem to know any more about COVID than you city-slickers. Masks, distancing, no buses, whatever."

They picked up pizza and Diet Cokes, and decided to eat outside, affording more privacy. For what, Jessica did not know.

"OK, Bowman, what's up?"

"Jess, I'm not sure how to tell you this, but there's an elephant in the room when we're together."

"We call that a matzo ball, Bo. What about it?"

"I think I'm gay!"

"You think? Is that supposed to make me feel any better?"

"I have thought about it for some time, and when you tried to kiss me, it concerned me. I think you are adorable, and you know I love you in that platonic way, but I did not respond physically."

"Have you *been* with anyone?"

"No, I'm scared shitless. I wouldn't know what to do, but Mr. Johnson here has responded to a couple of guys."

"Bo, I think it's about the same as with someone of the opposite sex, with the obvious limitations."

"I'll figure that out, Jessica, eventually, but I needed to talk to you about it. I value our friendship and am hoping this will not jeopardize it."

"Bo, I'll admit I wanted more but over the last several months I figured that won't happen. Now I guess I understand it. But we'll always be friends. This won't change that, and I appreciate you're confiding in me." Jessica placed her hand on Bo's in a platonic way. "Who else knows?"

"No one," he lied, "and I'd like to keep it that way as long as I can."

"Good by me, Bo."

They went back into the Market and bought a huge chocolate chip cookie to share at the Ultimate Bake Shoppe. Bo was targeting the 1:50 train. Ignoring COVID, they briefly hugged and went their separate ways.

Chapter 42

October 25, 2020

Since identifying Jason Rogers in August, Brahim Jones and Damian Mitchell had laid low, wanting to focus on the business when school reopened. While sales of the jawn had improved, it had not returned to the pre-COVID levels, and they knew it would not unless they shut down JRo's operation.

They hoped that would happen tonight. They had learned that Rogers lived in the 5700 block of Poplar Street. At 5:50, Heem parked his car on 57th Street. They walked up Poplar so they could see JRo's house with the binoculars Damian brought. They could never be certain that he would be leaving, but he didn't stay in many nights. If he left by car, they'd rush back to Heem's car and follow him. If he walked, they would tail him on foot.

Their plan was not elaborate. Heem had a gun with a silencer that he had gotten from Sheila Gates, Big Earl's cousin. Whether on foot or by car, they would wait until Rogers was alone, walk up to him and one shot in the head would do it. If that opportunity did not present itself, they would try again tomorrow night. COVID did have one thing in their favor, the surrounding foot traffic was lighter than usual.

They had started to wonder if tonight's plan would happen as it was approaching 7:30 and they had grown impatient. But at 7:20, the door opened and JRo came out. He lit up a cigarette and turned in their direction. They retreated to 57th Street, knowing he would have to go right or left on 57th. Either way presented opportunities; North would go by Carroll Park, South would go by Shepard Recreation Center. As an added bonus, it appeared that JRo was wearing headphones, most likely listening to loud music and not Pod Save America.

He headed South; the Rec Center was in play.

"Look Dame, you go get my car, bring it back, and park on Haverford Avenue. I'll follow Rogers and I'll do this within ten minutes or meet you back at the car. You stay in the driver's seat and slowly take off when I get in. No rushing off, just stay cool. You good?"

"I'm good Heem, be careful and stay cool yourself!"

They both crossed to the other side of 57th to observe. When JRo crossed Haverford Avenue, it was clear that he'd continue on 57th past the Rec Center. Damian took off toward the car and Heem decided to scoot down the block, cross 57th, and walk back toward Rogers. Heem's adrenaline was pumping overtime as he skulked toward Rogers. Trying not to look obvious, he continued glancing around to make certain no pedestrians or drivers were taking notice.

When he was within twenty-five yards, Heem quietly and discreetly removed the gun from his belt and held it behind his back. As they walked past each other, Heem stopped, placed the gun within six inches of Rogers' head, and squeezed. Pfft!

It was over. He placed the gun back into his belt and continued walking at a quick pace toward Haverford. He glanced back once and saw JRo on the ground, motionless and a slowly increasing pool of blood gathering.

Chapter 43

April 10, 2022

"Forgive me guys, but we are six weeks from Bo Campbell's trial and I'm no more comfortable than when we last met. Detectives, start from the top please, and tell me as if I were on the jury."

The District Attorney, David Kasper had again convened Michelle Pugh, Vernon Brown, and Roberta Rumson to his office on this high-profile case. The last update Pugh had given him was the witness claiming that Campbell and Claxton "appeared to be romantically involved."

Brown would take the lead on this; it was his investigation. "Claxton was found on the corner of 53rd and Osage, about two blocks from his home with two shots in the chest. Bo claims that they had been at The Palestra for the Villanova-LaSalle game. They had taken the subway home, Claxton got off at 52nd and Market, and Bo continued to 63rd Street. Bo claims it was about 11:00 and that jives with the discovery of the body at 11:20.

"We did not find anyone who was on the street. We talked to a few of the bar patrons and restaurant workers who were still open at that time, but they saw or heard nothing. Claxton was well known in the area and would have been recognized had he stopped. It could have been a random robbery but his wallet and $25 were still on his body. So was his cell phone, but few of those were stolen anymore.

"You pretty much know the rest. The next day an anonymous voicemail message is left on the Crime Stopper Hotline that evidence can be found in Bo Campbell's locker in school. We found the gun and heroin in the locker and went ahead and arrested Bo."

"Forensics or autopsy give anything?" Kasper asked.

Brown continued, "Nothing helpful. Confirmed that the gun was in fact the murder weapon but there were no fingerprints. Autopsy only confirmed the weapon but no drugs in the body and only a modest amount of alcohol. Bo said they each had two beers, as neither was driving.

Then, you know, that two weeks ago this Deforia Weeks comes in with his mother and claims that Bo and Claxton were gay."

Assistant DA Pugh asked, "Did anyone else know about the relationship?"

Rumson answered that one, "As best we can tell, two friends, Jessica Marks and Carl Watkins, knew for some time. Bo's family and attorney only learned recently, after the murder. Neither Watkins nor Marks could tell us anything about any falling out."

Kasper stood and started pacing around the table as he asked, "Michelle, I know our case, such as it is, what will be their narrative?"

Pugh replied, "On cross-exam, they'll impeach our testimony claiming that the evidence was planted and that the defendant's prints were not found on the weapon or jawn. They will most likely put on Marks and Watkins, who will admit the relationship but claim there was no problem, no breaking up, no conflict whatsoever between Campbell and the deceased."

"Should I even ask, do we have the right guy?" Kasper queried them all.

Brown raised his eyes almost in disbelief as he replied, "You know my answer, Dave."

Rumson replied, "I've been listening to Vernon for the last two months, so I think I should abstain."

Michelle said, "I'd rather plead their case."

Kasper asked, "Vern, are there any other leads? Someone killed this kid. If not Campbell, who?"

"The Narc Squad confirms that West Philly appears to have had a battle going on since Big Earl's death two years ago, and the murder of Jason Rogers two years ago. They've identified three distinct players, Brahim Jones, Pops Williams, and some unidentified guy. But none of the kids will, or can, confirm any of this. They have undercover students in Overbrook and West Philly but that takes time, time that we don't have right now."

An increasingly impatient Kasper added, "Michelle, if you feel otherwise let me know, but I believe if we don't have anything more solid by May 15th, we drop the charges. If we do, that'll put the heat on you, Vern, and Roberta. The city wants this murder solved."

"I don't disagree, Dave. We'll keep digging," Michelle added.

"Meeting adjourned."

Chapter 44

February 1, 2021

The holidays and the New Year had come and gone. COVID was a major factor in celebrations, but a vaccine rollout had begun for seniors and immune-compromised individuals. Everyone was holding their collective breath that the country had turned the corner on this pandemic.

The Philadelphia Public and Parochial Schools had postponed all sports, but an abbreviated basketball season was scheduled to begin on February 15th, and try-outs and practice started at Overbrook on January 15th. Bo Campbell knew that his junior year would be critical for him to impress colleges, but just as important to Bo was winning City and State Championships. Anything less than that would be unacceptable.

Bo and Sherman Claxton had consummated their relationship and Bo was conflicted; he truly cared for Sherman and was glad they had moved forward, but he was stressed about keeping this secret. He was relieved that Sherman felt the same way, but it was difficult for two 6'5" black kids to go unnoticed. There would be absolutely no PDAs and they met every couple of weeks at FDR Park down by the Sports Complex in South Philadelphia.

With schools back in session, so were the dope peddlers, and that meant Mr. B needed to replace Jason Rogers quickly or run the risk of losing business and customers to Heem Jones and this Pops guy. Since his anonymity remained critical, he couldn't just trust anyone. He reluctantly approached his nephew, Malcolm Newberry.

Mr. B knew he'd get shit from his sister, but he also knew that News was using. Since graduating from West Philly last June, Malcolm was only working part-time at the Target on City Avenue.

Newberry quickly connected with Garrett Green and Dwight Bridges at Overbrook and West Philly and had added one additional kid at each school. He was also ready to move forward with a kid at West Catholic. Newberry felt if he could add six more runners, he might be able to give up Target. Then again, how would he explain that to his mom?

There had been no new Tranq deaths in West Philly; Heem and Mr. B seemed to have gotten the message to Little Nicky Scarpatti that killing kids would destroy their businesses, and he needed to more closely supervise the cooking process.

Brahim Jones and Sheila Gates were meeting this morning at the Supreme Oasis Deli on Lancaster Avenue near the zoo. Supreme was one of those places tourists would never find out about. Nothing trendy about the location or the ambiance, the locals came for the food that ranged from the oxymoronic vegan cheesesteak to the Bean Pie Cheesecake. Despite the eclectic options, they both opted for Beyond Meat burgers and potato salad. They ordered and paid at the counter and found seats along the back wall.

"There's still things I don't understand about this business, Heem," Sheila began, "you got rid of that JRo character to eliminate competition, but I'm not seeing any increase in revenue. I'm thinking I'd be better off just running my girls and let you be the Drug King."

"You ain't wrong, Sheila. But offing JRo sent a message to not raid our guys. Dwight Bridges defected to JRo. Also, your johns want our jawn. Together we are full service providers. You're right that killing Rogers didn't end competition but we'll always have rivals. If we don't want a full-scale war, the best option for growth is to expand into the other schools where there is less competition."

"Are kids our only potential customers? Why can't we get some guys on the streets?"

"Worth looking at Sheila. I got a couple of guys I can talk to. Don't lose faith. This'll work now that COVID's behind us. I'll update you next week."

They walked out together and then went their separate ways.

Chapter 45

April 12, 2022

"Hey, Godfather, what's up?"

"I'm overdue for a donut, you hungry? See you at Dunkin' in fifteen minutes? I'm buying."

This was a typical call between James McNeil and his Godfather, Kenny Anderson. Kenny was his dad's best friend, and since his death, they had much more contact, which James loved. Kenny was much more plugged into the neighborhood doings and thus always a good source of information and rumors.

Late morning was always a good time as the coffee and donut crowd eased up. James arrived first but decided to wait for Kenny, since Kenny offered to pay, he would be pissed if James had ordered in advance. Two minutes later, Kenny walked in with a smile.

After they hugged, Kenny said, "OK young man, one coffee and one donut is the limit. Miss Brittney is waiting on you."

They took their goodies to a table by the window.

"This is your meeting, Godfather, whatta ya got?"

"I don't want to put you in an awkward position but I'll do that, regardless. You remember that high-stakes poker game your dad was involved with before he died, upstairs at the 601 Lounge?"

"Sure, I remember, Kenny, even though I knew nothing about it back then until you told me. What about it?"

"The owner of the bar, Jalen Moore, also often plays in the poker game. I was in there the other night, and he pulls me aside to tell me that your son-in-law has been playing the last couple of months, and he's been losing. He estimates he's lost fifty thousand dollars over that time."

"Ah, shit! Hugh ain't got that kind of money, Kenny. Two weeks ago, Winnie mentioned things being tight, but didn't want to worry me. The SOB is probably spending Bo's college money, thinking he'll win it back by the time Bo needs it next year. Gamblers live in a fantasy world. Their luck will change tomorrow, but tomorrow is always a day away."

"Profound James. Whatta you gonna do?" Kenny mumbled with a half-full mouth of donut.

"I'd like to kill the sonofabitch, but the timing ain't real good. I'll talk to him and see how bad this is. It's one thing if he borrowed from Bo's account, an entirely different thing if he's in deep to a Shark! I do appreciate your telling me though Kenny. I think I can get him to stop if I threaten to tell Winnie."

"Sounds like a plan. Good luck James."

"Hey, I got one for you. Do you remember Lamont Card? He was a year ahead of me at West Philly. I knew him to say hello, but we weren't good friends."

"Yeah, still lives over on Poplar Street, I believe. I see him every now and then. Would you believe we have the same cardiologist? What about him?"

"Do you think that his grandson is the Lewis Card who plays for West Philly?"

"It definitely is. He mentioned it two years ago, I think the kid was a freshman."

"Well then, he would have been a teammate of Sherman's. It might not hurt for me to talk to him, see what he might know about Sherman or the drug jawn at West."

"Why not let me set up lunch one day next week with Lamont? It will be less surprising for him to hear from me."

"Great, but the sooner the better, Kenny. The trial is only six weeks away."

"I'll be in touch, James. Take care."

"You too, Godfather, and thanks for the breakfast. I'll set up that lunch."

They both stood, removed their trash, and walked out onto 52nd Street together.

James hoped this would be a lead that would give them something. He was convinced that Sherman was killed by someone in the West Philly High drug culture. But first, he would need to have a chat with his son-in-law. *Shit!*

Chapter 46

March 10, 2021

Overbrook breezed through the abbreviated basketball schedule with only one loss, a one-point defeat at the hands of Edison High School when Bo had to sit out due to a stomach virus. A week ago, they defeated Central High for the Public League Championship and today, they were back at The Palestra to play Roman Catholic High for the City Championship. The Philly Public Schools decided when they resumed the abbreviated schedule, that they would not participate in the State Championship this year as it was feared that COVID was too much of a risk to have these kids traveling around the state.

This would be Bo's last game in his junior year. He upped his game this season and averaged twenty-two points per game while still rebounding, assisting, and playing strong defense. His grandfather, James McNeil, had agreed to be the contact for colleges, and he had heard from fifty already, including all the Big 5 schools except for Penn. Coach Rosen also mentioned talking to Penn State, Michigan, and Georgetown. Bo would visit about six of these schools this summer.

The Palestra was an iconic sports arena on the University of Pennsylvania campus. Opened in 1927, it had been called, "the most important building in the history of college basketball." In the '60s and '70s, the Big 5 Philadelphia colleges Penn, Villanova, Temple, St. Joseph's, and LaSalle, as well as nationally known visiting teams, played to sell-out crowds.

The local high schools were limited at The Palestra to two days in March: the Public and Catholic League Championship games, then a week later, the City Championship.

Roman Catholic went undefeated through the season and had their own Super Star, Sean O'Hanlon, the grandson of Lafayette coach,

Fran O'Hanlon. He was expected to be a formidable obstacle in Overbrook's quest for the championship.

The Palestra was filled to 80% capacity, with the student bodies of both schools well represented. But unaffiliated basketball fans also came out to see these two ballyhooed stars, and alumni of the local colleges were also curious to see who they hoped their schools might recruit. Bo's family sat with the other players' families in the three rows behind the bench. Sherman Claxton had come in for the game and was sitting with Claudia Campbell.

During warm-ups, the student bodies tried to out-scream each other but, with double the students, Overbrook won that battle. The players looked tense, not unexpected as most were playing in the biggest game of their young lives.

As the game began, the tightness remained, and, midway through the first quarter, the score was only 8-6 and both teams had committed four turnovers. But both teams warmed to the task as O'Hanlon hit two three-pointers and Bo had two dunks and a tip-in. At halftime, Roman led 35-31. Bo had twelve points, and O'Hanlon fourteen in their personal duel.

Coach Rosen addressed the team in the locker room, "I don't like our zone against these guys. It gives this O'Hanlon too many open shots from the perimeter. Bo, can you handle him, without affecting your offense?"

"You got it, Coach!"

Rosen held up his Surface Tablet and illustrated, "The rest of you match up by position and height. Bo will need help on picks so be quick to switch and then switch back as soon as you can. Let's zone press after we score, but back off into man-to-man at mid-court. We need to fast-break more off the rebounds. Outlet to Carl, then Bo, you fill the middle. And let's not be careless with the ball. Too many turnovers in that first half. No one has more than two fouls, so we are good there. Any questions?"

Silence. Each player was in his own thoughts. A good sign: these kids knew what they had to do.

As play resumed, the pace slowed as both teams were trying to read the other's halftime adjustments. The only immediately obvious one was Overbrook's man-to-man and Bo matching up with O'Hanlon.

Overbrook scored and quickly went into a press. They were rewarded when the Roman guard panicked and dribbled off his foot, out of bounds. Bo hit a quick jump shot on the inbounds play. They pressed again and Roman was called for a ten-second violation, failing to get the ball over half court. The Roman coach called a time-out, wanting to settle his kids down and remind them how to break the press.

Next time down court, Overbrook's Ron Jenkins scored off a give-and-go, and they pressed again. Roman was ready this time and got the ball over mid-court. But with ten seconds on the shot clock, they needed to hurry a shot. They got the ball to O'Hanlon at the top of the key, but Bo fought through a pick and O'Hanlon threw up a contested desperation shot. Overbrook got the rebound and quickly passed out to Carl on the wing. Bo filled the center, got the ball and at the key, feinted right, and drove down the middle for a dunk. The rout was on as the Roman coach called another timeout, and the Overbrook fans were going wild.

This timeout didn't help Roman much. With a fifteen-point lead, Bo got a breather late in the third quarter, but returned at the start of the fourth. Holding that lead, the Overbrook starters came out with three minutes left in the game, allowing them to be cheered on, and the reserve players some court time. The game ended with Overbrook winning 75-58, Bo leading all scorers with twenty-seven points; O'Hanlon had 21, only scoring seven in the second half against Bo's defense.

The typical on-court celebration seemed staged as the outcome had long been foreseen. Both teams shook hands and Bo and O'Hanlon spoke for a couple of minutes.

The fans had drifted onto the court and the players sought out their families. The school had set up a dinner. Win or lose, for the team and their families at the Sheraton Hotel on Chestnut Street, a short walk from The Palestra. After showers, the players and families would meet there.

The players were exhausted but jubilant in the locker room. The coach quickly congratulated them all and gave a special shout-out to the graduating seniors, including Carl Watkins. Bo hugged his friend, and said, "Way to go out, bruh. Great game."

They showered, dressed, and walked as a group over to the Sheraton.

Chapter 47

April 27, 2021

Hugh Campbell grew up in Chester, Pennsylvania, a city in Delaware County that sat on the Delaware River midway between Philadelphia and Wilmington, Delaware. Chester had a riches-to-rags story; William Penn first landed there in 1682 and thus it became the oldest city in Pennsylvania.

Chester evolved over the centuries from a small town with wooden shipbuilding and textile factories into an industrial city[1] producing steel ships for two World Wars and a myriad consumer goods. Since the mid-twentieth century, it had lost its manufacturing base and over half of its residents and devolved into a post-industrial city struggling with pollution, poverty, and crime. In 2022, the city declared bankruptcy. When asked where they came from, most residents offered "Delaware County," hoping that would suffice.

Campbell never knew his dad and wished he never knew his mom. She succumbed to a life of drugs and alcohol when he was ten. He then lived with his Aunt Maxine who supplied a no-frills, modest sense of security.

Hugh was a good student, but not great. After graduating from Chester High School, he obtained a Bachelor of Arts degree in Social Work from Delaware County Community College, moved in with a friend in Philly, and got a job with the city in the Social Services Division.

Five years later, he met Winnie McNeil in the SSD, a recent Temple graduate, and they had an immediate connection. They were married a year later, and their daughter, Claudia was born fifteen months later. With a little help from Winnie's dad, they bought the house they still live in today in the Wynnefield section of West Philadelphia. Their

---

1.   https://en.wikipedia.org/wiki/Industrial_city

neighbor, Mrs. Henderson, offered to babysit two days a week, and Winnie reduced her schedule. When Kenny was born, she quit altogether to be a full-time mom.

Social work had taken a toll on Hugh and, after ten years, he transferred to Licensing and Inspections, where he remained today. He had a decent salary and good benefits, but he dreamed of more. He was jealous of the McNeil family and, while they were generous with gifts and financial help, it made him feel that he was accepting charity.

Two years ago, Campbell had been offered a bribe to expedite the licensing of a building renovation. He turned it down, but started to wonder, *might this be a routine thing here in L&I?* Six months after that, when he was offered $5,000 in cash to ignore asbestos in an apartment building on Broad Street, Hugh accepted it. *Who would find out and everyone must be doing it*, he rationalized.

Hugh decided to keep these funds a secret from Winnie, as she no doubt would disapprove. And perhaps he could parlay this windfall into something more significant.

Chapter 48

April 15, 2022

Willie Heyward walked into the Cottontails Bar at 52nd and Spruce Streets. Two steps in, the owner, bartender, and dishwasher, Jack Shepard yelled, "Well look what the cat dragged in. Where the hell have you been, Willie?"

"Nice to be missed, Jack, but it looks like you haven't cleaned the place since I was last here. Throw me a towel will you so I can clean up before the Board of Health gets here."

Cottontails was a drinking man's bar. Ownership had changed three times in the last ten years, and neither owner had added much to the décor of contemporary Formica. The one large TV over the bar stayed tuned to Sports Center all decay unless a live game preempted it. Even though no smoking was permitted, there was a stench of beer and tobacco in the place, emanating from the customers who took their smoke breaks outside.

If someone wanted food, their choices were either roast beef or roast pork sandwiches, carved in front of them by the bartender; no extra charge for provolone, or the pickle. Bags of chips, Doritos, and Cheese Doodles were available from a wire rack.

It was 2:00 in the afternoon. Cottontails didn't do much of a lunch business, but they opened at eleven and someone was always at the bar. At this hour, one man was at the other end of the bar, and two men were in the middle. Two tables were occupied apparently by late lunch diners.

"What'll you have?" Shepard asked.

"Budweiser," Heyward responded, taking a seat down the far end of the bar.

When Shepard brought his beer, he asked Heyward, "Really, how long has it been since you were in?"

"I know exactly when it was. Two months ago, and it's why I stopped by today. It was the night that the Claxton kid got killed up on 53rd Street. I left here at about eleven. So, you know, from here I walk up to 53rd Street and then down to Webster. I seen two tall Black guys, and one might have been following the other. I'm sure the one being followed was that Claxton kid. He lives in the next block from me. You think it means anything?" Heyward took his first chug of beer, gulping a good third of the glass.

"The police were in here that night before I closed asking if I might know who was in the bar and if anyone might have seen or heard anything. We are two blocks from 53rd and Osage, so I just shrugged. You thinking of going to the police and telling them you saw two tall Black kids on the street? I'm not certain that will solve the case unless you can identify that Campbell kid."

"I think I should tell them and let them figure it out. It might at least confirm it was a tall Black kid."

"Guess you might be right, Willie, but have another beer on the house."

Heyward did that and, at 3:15, settled up, and walked toward 55th and Pine Streets.

Ten minutes later, he walked into the 18th District Police Station.

Heyward stepped up to the window and the desk sergeant asked, "May I help you, sir?"

"Yes, I may have some information about the Claxton murder, and I thought I should at least tell someone."

"Please have a seat, sir. I'll see if one of the detectives is in."

He rang Vernon Brown's number.

"Roberta Rumson, whatta you got, Sarge?"

"Hey Roberta, Vern not in?"

"Nah, can I help?"

"I have a fellow down here. Claims he might know something about the Claxton murder. You want to talk to him?"

"Absolutely. Be down in five. Put him in the conference room please."

Five minutes later, she entered the small conference room. A round table with four chairs, a small lamp on the table, and a picture of the mayor and police chief were the extent of the decoration.

Poised with her notebook, Rumson said, "Good afternoon, I'm Detective Rumson, may I ask your name?"

"Sure, Willie Heyward."

"Mr. Heyward, can I get you some coffee or water? That's about all I can offer?"

"No thank you. I'm good."

"I understand you may have some information related to the Sherman Claxton murder. Tell me about it, please. I'd like to record this conversation, not for court or as evidence, just for my partner. Is that OK?"

"Sure. First, let me tell you that I cannot positively identify anyone, and even then, I cannot be sure the man I saw was the killer. I had been at Cottontails that night. I left at about eleven and walked over to 53rd Street on my way home."

"Excuse me, can I have your address, Mr. Heyward?"

"Sure, 5417 Webster Street."

"Continue, please."

"The street is quiet. And then I see a tall kid coming toward me. We glanced at each other and we both continued walking. Then about forty yards behind him, another tall dude was walking in the same direction."

"I noticed you said 'tall kid' and then 'tall dude'?"

"The first one's face was clear, and he was a kid or a teenager. But I couldn't see much of the face on the second one. He was wearing one of those knit caps and his coat collar was up. He also didn't look at me, his head was toward the street. With hindsight, he might have been hiding his face from me."

"Are you certain the first kid was Sherman Claxton?"

"Ninety-nine percent certain! He lives in the neighborhood, and I had seen him before. When I passed him, something registered but it wasn't until I heard he had been murdered that I realized that's who I had seen."

"And why did you wait two months to come in?"

"I didn't want to get involved or accuse someone that I really never got a good look at. Over the last week or two, I had been thinking and today I went back to Cottontails for the first time since that night. Talking with Jack Shepard, we both agreed that I should at least give you this information, and you can decide if it is relevant."

"You said they were both tall. Can you say how tall, and was one taller than the other?"

"Once again, I ain't real certain here, but I'm certain that Claxton was shorter than the other fella, who might have been two-three inches taller."

"Notice anything else, clothing, glasses, shoes?"

"Nah! My wife says that I am the most unobservant man alive, and you should be lucky I noticed they were males."

"I think that is about it, Mr. Heyward. As you may know, the trial is scheduled for next month. If the District Attorney needs you to testify, someone will be in touch with you. I do appreciate your coming in." They both stood, shook hands, and Rumson showed him out.

Rumson at once placed a call to Vernon Brown, but got his voicemail, "Hey Vern, Roberta here, give me a call ASAP."

Chapter 49

June 10, 2021

Brahim Jones and Sheila Gates were back at the Supreme Oasis Deli having the same burger and potato salad lunch.

"Whatever you've done, Heem, seems to be working as our numbers are looking much better. Care to share?"

"I let things coast at Overbrook and West Philly, but added second runners at West

Catholic, St. Joe's, and two more working both Penn and Drexel. The results have been good. Funny, college kids seem to favor old favorites like weed and blow, while the high school kids are more adventurous. No ODs, which is a good thing. And I put someone on the street down at Mt. Vernon Park area in Mantua to get some non-student business as you suggested, Sheil."

"And how about Pops and JRo's former guys?"

"I'm not certain, but I believe that Pops decided to keep his focus in the Southwest. He may be thinking there is too much competition here in West Philly. That's the good news. The bad is that JRo was quickly replaced by a kid who goes by the name of News. I know nothing about him and still believe he is fronting for someone. Damian and Spooky are watching the situation there, but the market seems stable. I'm not anxious to handle this News dude like we did JRo. It did not get us the results we wanted."

"I agree Heem. Since the COVID situation eased, the girls are back to where they were, so that's all good. No supply issues?"

"All seems good there too, Sheila."

"Sounds good, Heem. Stay in touch, my brother." They got up together and walked out.

Hugh Campbell's blood pressure had been building for months now. When Bo started his junior year, Hugh had expected to be the point man and represent Bo with recruiters and his college selection process. But somehow, Bo's grandfather James had worked his way into that position. James meant well, but he was so damn controlling; he always knew best about everything, and Winnie rarely challenged her dad. With college visits to be scheduled this summer, now was the time to confront the situation.

Bo was having dinner with Jessica somewhere, so it was only Hugh and Winnie at home.

"Win, we need to talk. I've been holding this in, but I'm pissed that your dad seems to be Bo's agent. I expected to be representing Bo with the colleges. And now with college visits to be scheduled, does James expect to be going with Bo and calling all the shots?"

"Hugh, I actually thought you welcomed my dad's involvement, with your work, and his availability. You know that James had a connection to Jay Wright at Villanova and that just started it, I guess. Ultimately it will be a family decision with Bo getting the last word. What do you want me to do?"

"I'm not really sure. I don't want to put you at odds with your dad. Maybe we might share this, divvying up the schools?"

"Look, Dad ain't crazy about flying anyway, and Bo wants to go visit Gonzaga and UCLA, so you and he can schedule that. Let Dad handle Villanova and any other of the drivable visits. If Bo wants to go to Kansas or Michigan, you can do that. If you're OK with this, I'll discuss it with my dad."

"Seems like a good plan. I knew you'd know how to best handle it. Thanks, Hon!"

Hugh wasn't 100% satisfied, suspecting that James might not welcome sharing his role, but for now, it would do.

Chapter 50

June 15, 2021

It was the first day of summer for Bo Campbell and all the rest of the Philadelphia public school students, whose last day was yesterday. Sherman had been home from Widener for three weeks now. Philly schools were always the last to end their school year.

Bo had a busy schedule planned. He had signed up to play in the Narberth League again and Sherm had talked him into volunteering a couple of days at the Haddington Playground. And of course, he'd be visiting maybe six or more colleges. Villanova, North Carolina, and Gonzaga seem to be leading the chase, but Bo was intrigued with two other schools because of their coaches: Shaka Smart at Marquette and Jim Larrañaga at Miami. Wisconsin was a negative for Marquette; Bo could not imagine going to a place colder than Philadelphia, not when he had other warm-weather options.

Bo received a nice surprise from the family yesterday: Claudia's 2018 Corolla. She was upgrading to a new RAV4, and, rather than trade it in, the family bought it from her to give to Bo. *No more subway or begging for rides here and there. INDEPENDENCE,* Bo thought.

He had big plans today. First, he would wash and detail the car, then pick up Carl and head out to Hymie's Delicatessen in Merion to meet Jessica. Maybe they would take a ride out to Villanova and peruse the campus.

School is out at last, and I'm so happy I passed, Bo sang to himself.

Assistant coach Reggie McIntosh grew up on North 11th Street in North Philadelphia, the youngest of three children of Trudy and William McIntosh. Neither had graduated high school. Bill drove a SEPTA bus and Trudy worked part-time at a nearby CVS. They were hard-working, church-going kind of people who wanted their kids to have better, but raising kids in North Philadelphia was never easy. Poverty, crime, and drugs were a fact of daily life.

Reggie's older brother had been killed by gunfire at the age of fourteen. They never found out for certain if he was in a gang, or just a bystander. *Why did it matter now*? Reggie and his sister Claudette both attended nearby Benjamin Franklin High School. Reggie got decent grades and played basketball in his junior and senior years at Franklin. At 6' 1", he wasn't tall enough to play forward and his perimeter shooting was so-so, thus his playing time was limited as the third guard.

In his senior year, his sister confided in him that she was a lesbian. He was uncomfortable knowing this; maybe because he didn't know anyone else who was gay. He thanked Claudette for telling him and agreed to keep this confidential but pleaded with her not to give him any more details.

Needing spending money, Reggie did some drug running for the *Frankies*, a small-time drug gang dealing mostly in weed and oxy. He had to sample the merchandise but did so cautiously and never got hooked.

Thanks to a special program at Temple University that compromised admission and tuition requirements for intercity kids, Reggie enrolled there as an Education Major. He thought he would be a Physical Education teacher in high school and perhaps do some basketball coaching on the side.

In 2006, Reggie graduated from Temple and got a job at Roxborough High School teaching Physical Education and was an assistant coach on the Junior Varsity basketball team. Three years later, he became head coach of the JV team and assistant coach of the Varsity Team. In 2012, Big Mac, as he was now known, made a lateral move to Bartram High School in the Southwest section of the city. And, in 2018, he transferred to his current position at Overbrook High School.

At Bartram, Big Mac had met a fellow by the name of Pops Williams. Pops was running a drug operation in Southwest Philly and parts of bordering Delaware County. Mac was interested in supplementing his income but did not want to work for Pops. Williams said that so long as Mac stayed out of his territory, he would introduce him to his suppliers. Mac agreed to this, asking Pops what he knew about West Philadelphia.

"What goes around, comes around, Mac. Big Earl Jackson, a former associate of mine, is running the schools in West Philly. I have thought about expanding there, but go ahead if you want, take a shot. I started growing Delco, so my plate is full."

"I might look into that. Thanks, Pops!"

Chapter 51

April 16, 2022

Roberta Rumson had updated Vernon Brown about Willie Heyward's visit. Brown wanted to dismiss it, but of course, any possible identification of Bo would lend itself to the DA's narrative.

He placed a call to Michelle Pugh.

"Hi Vernon, got something?"

"A big maybe, Michelle. Guy by the name of Willie Heyward walked into the station yesterday. Roberta spoke with him, and he claimed to be certain he saw a tall, Black man following Claxton on 53rd Street the night of the murder. Said he did not get a good look at the guy, but he was taller than Claxton."

"Not exactly a smoking gun, is it Vern? If we are going to trial, we'll need to subpoena and interview him."

"He's been prepared for that, Michelle."

"Thanks, Vern, I'll be in touch."

Since the defense would learn of this anyway, Brown decided to call James McNeil with the heads-up, leaving out only Heyward's name.

As was becoming the pattern, James called his granddaughter Claudia, who in turn called Melanie Wexler.

"Yo girl," Melanie answered, "What's up?"

"Not great news, but it could be worse. Some guy in West Philly told the police he was on 53rd Street the night of the murder, and he saw a tall Black guy following Claxton shortly after 11 PM."

"Did he ID Bo?"

"Nope, said he didn't get a good look at him, only that he was a couple inches taller than Claxton."

"You're right. It could be worse. While I got you, any plans for the weekend?"

"I got tickets for a concert on Saturday night, but I'm OK for Friday. You want to come out this way? I'll make a reservation for seven. Meet me at my place, six forty-five?"

"Sounds good, Claudia. See you then."

Claudia gave her the address, and they disconnected.

James and Kenny picked up Lamont Card at 11:45, and they decided they'd go to Dibbs Barbecue on Lancaster Avenue, two blocks from Overbrook High. It had been raining hard all morning and no let-up was in sight. The only concession to the rain was that they each had a hat on, a Phillies, an Eagles, and a beret.

When Card got into the back seat of James's Lexus RX350, he exclaimed, "James McNeil, long time no see, my brother. All good by you? Sorry about Bo. How's that going?"

"Being under house arrest and the trial getting closer, he's going crazy, Lamont. We'll talk about that at lunch. How are you and your family?"

"I think you know I lost my wife Shirley two years ago. We had both stopped smoking five years ago, but the damage had been done, at least for her. She lugged an oxygen tank around for the last two years of her life. Nasty stuff, those cigarettes. I heard you finally retired?"

"Yeah, been four years now, shortly before my dad died. I think Rasheed is doing a great job with PhillyBeats, in fact, better than me, but if you tell him that, I'll put a hurtin' on you."

"Your secret is safe with me, James."

James parked outside Dibbs', and they dashed in, shook off the rain, and took a booth along the far wall. Only a couple of tables were occupied. James knew Diggs did a big dinner and takeout business, but apparently, people were eating lighter for lunch. The décor was dinerish, with five booths running down both sides and six tables spaced out in the middle. There was counter seating for six next to the takeout pick-up station.

There was no bar, but bottled beer was available. All three opted for Diet Cokes. When the server brought them, she asked, "Would you like to order, or do you need more time?"

Reading from her name tag, James replied, "Could we have a few more minutes, Violet? We're in no hurry."

"You got it," she said and hurried off to check on other customers.

Kenny had been quiet but now said, "As I mentioned on the phone, Lamont, James has been looking into Claxton's murder to try and help Bo's lawyers get him acquitted. We thought catching up with you might be helpful. James."

"It was a good excuse to see you, Lamont, and this might be a long shot. I hear your grandson is playing for West Philly?"

"Lewis just finished his junior year and got more playing time this season. He's hopeful of starting next year, and maybe getting a scholarship to a smaller school, somewhere like Cheyney. He's no Bo Campbell, but he's got a pretty good game."

"That's great, Lamont. I wish him well. He would have been a freshman when Sherman Claxton played there. I assume he knew him?"

"He did know him, but I don't believe they were close. The age difference had them running in different circles. He did go to the funeral and mentioned seeing Bo there."

"My working theory is that Claxton may have learned something about drug activity at school, or maybe Overbrook, something he wasn't supposed to and was killed because of that. I'm not suggesting Lewis was involved in the drug scene, but these kids all seem to know the kids that are and their sources. I'd love to be able to speak with him."

Violet returned and took their orders.

Before they started chowing, Lamont replied, "I, of course, would have to speak with my son, but I think he'll be OK with this. He might want to be with you, but I'll talk to him tonight. I assume you'd like to do this ASAP?"

"Yeah, the trial is scheduled to start in five weeks, so this is rather urgent. Thanks, Lamont."

Small talk resumed; the Phillies were off to a slow start as usual, the Eagles loss in the Super Bowl, the rainy weather, crime in the city, and *HoagieFest at Wawa*.

Ten minutes later, Violet delivered their platters, ribs for Kenny, a rib and chicken combo for James, and a burger for Lamont; all came with fries and coleslaw. She also brought them drink refills.

They got down to the business of devouring the barbecue and the conversation was minimal.

They passed on dessert, and James settled the check with Violet. The rain had let up slightly, but they dashed to the car.

They said their farewells, and Lamont again said he would call James tomorrow.

Chapter 52

April 18, 2022

Claudia had made a reservation at Pescatore, a BYO Italian restaurant in Bala, not far from her apartment on the bank of the Schuylkill River. Perhaps she was cheap, but she hated paying $40 for a $15 bottle of wine, so she loved BYOs, and they were plentiful in the Philadelphia suburbs as liquor licenses were scarce and expensive.

She noticed the last time that Melanie drank a Cabernet Sauvignon, so she had picked up an Oyster Bay Australian one, which she heard was trendy now.

Melanie had texted her when she got off at the City Avenue exit, so she was less than five minutes away. Claudia thought she would meet her downstairs, let her drive, and then invite her up for dessert after dinner. She had gone out to The Bakery House in Bryn Mawr where the cakes and pies were to die for. She was able to get two halves, one of Apple Pecan Caramel, and the other of Key Lime. Whatever they did not eat, she would take to her mom and dad's tomorrow.

She got a mani and pedi today and chose a royal blue above-the-knee dress. She finished off with blue and silver jewelry and her best, and only, pair of Jimmy Choos. *Not bad*, she thought to herself.

A minute after she got Melanie's text, she jumped into Melanie's car and told her of her plan; fine by Melanie, and off they went. It was a mild night for mid-April, and she now regretted not choosing one with outdoor seating. Whatever! They parked on Bala Avenue, about a hundred yards from the restaurant.

Claudia had requested a table for two in the rear of the small, always-congested dining room and it was waiting for them. She also requested Christine to be their server. As they sat, the busboy filled their water glasses and dropped off bread with garlic aioli butter.

Christine flew by delivering entrees to a table of four, but stopped quickly to say, "Hey Claudia, nice to see you, I'll be right there to open your wine."

"You're a regular here, huh?" Melanie asked.

"How often must one come to be considered a *regular*? I'd say I'm here once a month or so and, about six months ago, Christine was my server and we hit it off, so I ask for her when I think of it."

As promised, Christine returned promptly and began opening the wine bottle, she said, "Hey again, Claudia, how's everything? Your brother's trial starts soon, doesn't it?"

"Good memory, Christine. This is Melanie, she's Bo's attorney. Mel, this is Christine."

"Hi, Christine, good to meet you."

"You guys are here on a strategy session, huh? Good luck! Good news is we are not out of anything, and we've added to the menu tonight an *Eggplant Parmesan* served over linguini. I'll give you a few minutes. Take your time. Any questions?"

Melanie asked, "Just how hot is the *Lobster Fra Diavolo*?"

"It's quite hot, but we can dial it back for you if you would like. Or I can bring ice cream for dessert along with it." She left them to ponder the menu.

"I guess we should look at menus first," Melanie said, "Any suggestions?"

"Everything's good here. I hope we can share the *Flatbread Caesar Salad*, other than that, just go for it."

"Narrows it down, Claudia, but not much. I'm good with that Flatbread. I'll need to think more about my entrée."

They put the menus down and toasted.

"Nice wine. Thanks. I like this place, good suggestion."

"It's noisy and crowded, but intimate at the same time. Anything new on the case?"

"You know about this new witness if you can call him that. I spoke with Michelle in the DA's office, and she's not even certain she wants him to testify. On cross, she knows Fred would crush him on his uncertainty about everything."

"Your investigator come up with anything helpful?"

"Not really, Claudia, but he'll keep digging right up to and through the trial."

"New subject. Working on anything else exciting?"

"We're defending that City Councilman who was indicted on bribery charges. I suspect Fred will plead him out. He's guilty as sin. How about you?"

"I got an interesting case. Have you ever heard of a Life Insurance Settlement?"

"Not until you told me about your grandfather's murder."

"Get this: three months ago, my client's father sold his one million dollar life insurance policy to some investment firm and received five hundred grand for it. Two weeks ago, his father died. My client and his sister were the beneficiaries. They'll share the five hundred thousand that their father still had, but had he not sold the policy, they would have received an additional five hundred grand."

"Whom are you suing, and what's your case?"

"Anyone and everyone; the broker, investment firm, and the insurance company. We'll plead that he was coerced or tricked into selling the policy, and everyone except their dad made money on this scam."

"I like your case. The life insurance company, and I suspect the E&O carriers for the investment firm and broker, will settle. Keep me posted."

Christine stopped back and took their orders, the *Pescatore pasta* for Claudia and the *Lobster Fra Diavolo,* spice dialed down for Melanie.

The women relaxed, enjoying the wine and conversation. They were able to tune out everything and everyone around them.

Onlookers would see two attractive, professional women, enjoying their night out sans men.

The runner delivered the Flatbread appetizer, and Christine stopped back to refill the wine. Twenty minutes later, the entrees were delivered, and Melanie exclaimed. "Wow, everything looks great. Bon Appetit!"

As they ate, they covered the full spectrum of subjects: families, movies, books, vacations, and the current political mess. After the busboy had removed their plates, Christine asked about dessert and coffee and Claudia reminded Melanie that she had planned that for her place. They both threw out credit cards and asked Christine to split the bill in half.

"Wow, that was awesome, Claudia. I'm stuffed," Melanie said as they got into her car.

"You better make room for dessert, girl."

Claudia directed Melanie back to her apartment, and she parked in the designated visitor space. Claudia lived on the fourth floor, corner unit.

Upon entering, Melanie exclaimed, "Very nice, Claudia. Did you decorate yourself?"

"Mostly, with help from my mom and a friend of mine. I love it here."

She had two great views: the Schuylkill River and the hills of Manayunk to the north, and the river and Philadelphia skyline to the east. Furnishings were eclectic; contemporary furniture but a lot of family photos, as well as Philadelphia and Gullah artwork.

"Wine, coffee, or tea?"

"Coffee if convenient, please."

Claudia set up dessert at the counter and started the first cup in the Keurig. Both of them used the bathroom and returned with makeup freshened. Claudia turned on the stereo and a John Coltrane CD. They sat next to each other, Claudia cut the pies, and both selected small slivers of each.

When they had finished dessert, they made second cups of coffee and moved to the sofa. Melanie asked, "Is jazz your favorite music genre?"

"That and Motown. Picked up from my dad and grandfather. Jazz for listening, The Temptations for kicking."

Melanie inched closer to Claudia and asked, "Would you mind if I gave you a hug?"

"Well, OK. What's that about?"

"I just feel really close to you, Claudia. I'm so glad we've become friends."

"Me too, Mel."

Melanie embraced Claudia and held on longer than Claudia expected. Claudia's heart was beating a mile a minute, but it felt good to have a moment of intimacy with Melanie. When Melanie let go, she stayed close and took Claudia's hands. They leaned back, both silent but comfortable. *What is happening here*, Claudia thought to herself.

After a minute or two, they looked into each other's eyes, and Claudia embraced Melanie. She could feel Melanie's breath on her ear. Her body was responding to the closeness and the emotion. Claudia didn't know what was happening, but she had no desire to stop it. Melanie had placed her hand behind Claudia's head, and whispered in her ear, "This feels so good, Claudia."

"Please don't stop," was about all Claudia could blurt out.

Melanie slowly moved on top and straddled Claudia. She continued stroking her hair and nibbling on her ear. Claudia was now stroking Melanie's breast. As she moaned, she pulled her face four inches from Claudia's, stared into her eyes, opened her mouth, and kissed her. Their tongues played together, and Melanie bit the inside of Claudia's lip.

Melanie slid off and placed her hand under Claudia's dress while Claudia worked her hand under Melanie's bra and was caressing her nipple. Melanie was gently massaging Claudia's silk thong and could feel the wetness. Claudia moved first, slowly standing, and taking Melanie's hand. "Let's get more comfortable," she said and led her to her bedroom.

Chapter 53

October 1, 2021

Bo had a good summer. He limited his playing time in the Narberth Playground league, but he still felt his game was improving. He was doing some weight training to go with his running and felt stronger.

He and his dad had visited Gonzaga and UCLA, which were both great but decided to pass on Kansas and Michigan; much too cold in the winter. They still planned to visit Miami over Thanksgiving break, but truth be told, he was leaning toward Villanova. His family would be delighted to be able to attend all his home games, and thanks again to his dad and grandad, he had been a Villanova fan for the last ten years. True, Jay Wright had just announced his retirement as Head Coach, but everyone expected his designated successor, Kyle Neptune, to continue the legacy.

His new car gave him freedom; he and Carl made the rounds to the local Philly playgrounds and played in pick-up games. These games made him tougher, and they were competitive, with only the most flagrant fouls being called.

With Sherman working at Widener for the summer, taking a couple of classes, and practicing with two other teammates, he and Bo only got to see each other every three or four weeks. The relationship was solid, if not hot and heavy.

Bo continued to think about being gay. *How did that happen to me? I had wondered about my wiring; did it have anything to do with seeing all these naked, sweaty dudes in the locker room? And why did I respond to Sherman? Was it simply because he made himself available?*

Bo, Carl, and Jessica were often a threesome that everyone seemed fine with. In addition to the usual hanging, they took in a couple of Phillies games, one on Dollar Dog Night when Bo ate seven, Carl eight, and Jessica the wimp, only four. They made a couple of day trips to the Jersey shore, too.

Overbrook would start practice in three weeks for Bo's senior year. Bo had met with Coach Rosen two weeks ago, and they agreed that with the pressure off Bo, he could revert to his 15/15/15 strategy unless the game was close and he needed to take charge. Winning the Public and City Championships remained the non-negotiable goals.

Things were mostly good with Bo, except he was concerned that his mom and dad were arguing more, occasionally heated. He tried not to listen, but it sounded like it was about money. They had always lived comfortably if not extravagantly, but it sounded like his dad was spending on some things his mom disapproved of.

Hugh Campbell was now playing poker two to three times a week. He lost as much as he won. Actually, he lost more. He still had some private funds set aside, but he had started asking Winnie to be more frugal with their spending. Between his nights out and his concern about money, Winnie had begun nagging Hugh. These funds that he had accepted from contractors were not amassing the nest egg Hugh had expected.

He thought that he might solve both problems by cutting back to one night and making that a high-stakes game night. He had heard about one upstairs at the 601 Lounge. He went one night and sat at the bar with a drink, watching the activity from 6:30 to 7:00. He watched eight guys go upstairs; two he recognized as being high rollers, possibly drug guys, but he didn't know either of their names.

Hugh decided to ask the bartender, "How does one get into the game upstairs?"

"What game would that be?"

"We playing that game, like how do I know there's a game up there?"

Handing him a pad, the bartender said, "Write down your name and cell phone number. Someone will get back to you."

Hugh did, thanked him, and left.

There was quiet tension in the West Philadelphia drug war. Malcolm Newberry, Mr. B's nephew, had gotten aggressive and recruited Crazy Eddie Baxter to run at Overbrook, and Sneaky Pete Preston at West Philly, again cutting into the profits of Brahim Jones and Sheila Gates, but they had more than compensated with an increased presence at West Catholic High, Saint Joe's, Drexel, Penn Universities, and the streets of Mantua.

While Heem and Sheila may have been pleased, the lower volume in Overbrook and West Philly pissed off Spooky Little, Spanky Waters, Donovan Moore, and Damian Mitchell, who saw their personal incomes drop. The four of them had met without Heem's knowledge and discussed their options. No decision was made, but they agreed to meet again in November.

Chapter 54

April 20, 2022

Lamont Card had gotten back to Kenny Anderson and had set up a meeting at 4:00 with Lewis Card and his father, Lorenzo, at their house on the four thousand block of Olive Street. James McNeil picked up Kenny at 3:45 to make the short drive to the Card's.

They found parking five houses up and walked back. Father and son were sitting on the porch. The neighborhood was quiet except for six kids playing touch football in the street. As they approached the patio, Lewis and Lorenzo stood to greet them. Introductions were made, and they chose seats.

James knew he needed to lead this discussion and started, "Thanks for seeing us. I really appreciate it. As your dad explained, I'm trying to help my grandson's investigation. We all believe that whatever happened to Sherman Claxton was somehow drug-related. I understand that you knew Sherman, Lewis?"

"I did, Mr. McNeil. He was two years ahead of me, so we played together for two years. I didn't play much as a freshman, but I increased my playing time each year since. We didn't hang out together unless it was a team function, but I liked Sherman. He was a solid player and willing to help the newer guys like me."

"I understand that Sherman had experimented with drugs. Were you or any of his teammates aware of this?"

Lorenzo Card decided he needed to contribute, "Just so we understand each other here, my son is not involved with drugs in any way, and this conversation is off the record, not to be disclosed to anyone. Are we clear?"

"Absolutely, Lorenzo. I'm trying to learn what I can about the players in the local drug scene. You have our total confidence."

Lorenzo nodded and looked toward his son with an implied approval to answer.

"I did not know if or what Sherman might have tried. I know that several of the guys, including myself, had tried weed. I didn't care for it and told my mom and dad. I'm sure a couple of the guys might have continued using it but never around the team. If Coach Connelly had ever gotten a whiff of weed, he'd have suspended us all and forfeited the season."

"Any idea who the kids are selling the stuff?"

"I asked one of my teammates where he got his stuff; he got weed from two kids, Damian Mitchell or Pete Preston."

"I've heard that name Mitchell before."

"Yeah, he's been around a couple of years. This Sneaky Pete kid seemed to appear within the last six months."

Kenny Anderson had been quiet until now but said, "Could you ask your teammate where he met with Sneaky Pete? We can stake that out, confront Sneaky, and extort him to give up his supplier. That would move us one step up the hierarchy."

"I would be OK with that, so long as my teammate's name is never mentioned. OK with you, Dad?"

Lorenzo said, "Without putting Lewis at risk, I'd be glad to have him help clean up the drug situation at the school, so it sounds OK to me, but how you guys gonna squeeze this Pete kid? You ain't cops. The kid might put a hurtin' on you right there."

James said, "We ain't as frail as we look, Lorenzo, but I think we'll use the threat of turning him in for persuasion. These kids want to make some easy money but want to avoid complications like the police."

James wrote down his cellphone number and handed it to Lewis. "Call me with the location. I'll make certain to keep you and your teammate out of this. I sincerely appreciate this. Thank you both."

They all stood, shook hands, and thanked each other again.

Chapter 55

December 5, 2021

Bo had picked up Jessica, and they were heading down to Widener for Sherman's first game of the season. Widener was playing their cross-town rival Neumann College for the Championship of Chester. They were on the Blue Route I-476 that ran north and south in the Philly suburbs.

It was mild for early December, and Bo and Jessica could get by in sweatshirts and jeans; she had her Lower Merion sweatshirt on, Bo his Overbrook. They had not seen each other since school started but texted daily.

Bo asked, "How's Neil doing? Did Lafayette play their first game yet?"

"No, Wednesday night, they are coming down to The Palestra to play Penn. Wanna come?"

"Absolutely. I hope to play a couple of games there myself in March. Did I hear that Fran O'Hanlon is finally retiring as their coach?"

"Yep, after 27 years. He's a legend there."

"My great-grandfather actually saw him play at Villanova in the 60s. He said if they had had the three-point shot back then, he might have been a superstar." Bo was fidgeting, looking at the street signs as he knew his exit was soon, and did not want to miss it.

When he got his bearings, he asked, "Neil make his medical school plans as yet?"

"Yep, he's all set for Jefferson. I'm glad he's staying close. When's your first game?"

"A week from Tuesday, we open at Lincoln, and then Friday we are at home against Bartram. Sherm said he might come up for that. How about you?"

"We'll see. Speaking of Sherm, how's the romance going?"

"Cute Jess! OK, I guess, I got no experience with this stuff, and with the secrecy shit, I think we are both feeling our way through it."

They were quiet the rest of the way. Their timing was good, they arrived fifteen minutes before the 4:00 tip-off. They picked up the tickets that Sherm had arranged for them at the Will Call window and found their seats with Sherm's parents and sister. Bo introduced Jessica. They had left Bo the aisle seat so he could stretch his legs.

Five minutes later, the teams came out for their pre-game warm-up. Bo stood to cheer and felt a tug on his sweatshirt. He looked down to see a young girl of about ten with braids and a Widener sweatshirt, and sat down to be closer to her. She said, "My dad says you are Bo Campbell. Are you?"

"I am!"

"Can I have your autograph, please?" handing him her program and a pen. "My dad said it'll be worth a lot of money someday."

"I'm not sure about that, but I will sign your program. What's your name?"

"Halle."

"H-A-L-E-Y?"

"No, H-A-L-L-E!"

Bo signed, "TO MY FRIEND HALLE, THANK YOU FOR ASKING, BO CAMPBELL."

She thanked him and ran back to show her dad.

Jessica could not ignore this. "Wow! I didn't know I was sitting with someone famous. Can I get one of those?" mockingly rolling up her sleeve for Bo to sign.

"Very funny!"

The game started, and Widener jumped out to a quick 12-4 lead and coasted, winning the game 78-63, but the game was not as close as the final score. Sherman scored fifteen points and played well.

Bo asked Mr. Claxton, "How long will it be before they are dressed?"

"About a half hour, my guess. Coach will make a few comments, then showers. Would you and Jessica want to join us for dinner? We are going over to Pizzeria Uno, glad to have you."

Jessica and Bo had previously decided they'd head back and grab something in Bryn Mawr. Bo offered, "Thank you for the invite, Mr. Claxton, but I think we'll say hello and goodbye to Sherm and head home."

Forty minutes later, Sherm appeared outside, greeted everyone with hugs, Bo and Jessica said goodbye to all, and headed home.

Chapter 56

December 6, 2021

Six weeks ago, Hugh Campbell passed the entrance exam for admission to the poker game. The exam included how he had heard about the game, the privacy of the game, the individuals involved, and the stakes and game rules.

He had played four times since then and was down $15,000. Not exactly what he had hoped for, but he was starting to adjust to the game and the players. While poker was a game of chance and largely dependent on the cards you are dealt, every player had tendencies, habits, and tell signs, and the player who could read his opponents the best often prevailed, even without always having the best hand.

Of course, all players wanted to think they alone excelled in reading players, but Hugh had to admit to himself that thus far, he fell short. He had won $2,500 two weeks ago and felt good about the future.

Spanky, Spooky, Damian, and DWash decided that they would confront the newest runners, Crazy Eddie at Overbrook and Sneaky Pete at West, threaten them with a knife at the neck, and find out who their suppliers were. They had not decided once they got a name whether to involve Heem or deal with it on their own.

Damian and DWash were following Sneaky Pete after dismissal at West Philly. Sneaky walked down 49th Street toward Walnut Street. They knew Walnut would be too busy for any confrontation and hoped that was not his final destination. He crossed Walnut and made a left. A half a block later, he turned right onto Hanson Street, a street neither had heard of before. This was a quiet street, so they quickened their pace; they wanted to grab him before he got to his house, if that was where he was headed.

Damian grabbed Pete by the mouth while DWash put his arms around his waist. Damian held a knife to his throat and said, "We don't want to hurt you, Petey. I'll remove my hand from your mouth. If you scream or make any attempt to get away, you'll be found here by your neighbors, understand?"

Pete was struggling without success to break the hold and was only able to mumble an OK. Damian slowly removed his hand. "We only want to know who is supplying your stuff. He'll never know we got his name from you. Now talk!"

Squirming again to break loose, Petey said, "Look, I only know him as News. My buddy Dwight said I could make some easy money and no one would get hurt. I don't want no trouble. Please let me go."

Tightening his hold, Damian said, "And where do you meet this News?"

"Usually, the mart on 49th Street. I text him what I need. We meet and exchange backpacks, that's it. Quick and not much chatting."

"Good enough, Petey. That wasn't too difficult, was it? Not a word of this to anyone, including Dwight, you understand?"

"If Dwight or News finds out, I'm dead. I won't say a word, I swear, but you better not."

"We are men of our word Petey. There is no need for us to out you. Now, get home." Damian released his hold on Petey and waited for him to take off.

Chapter 57

April 22, 2022

James McNeil was on his way over to meet again with Lewis Card and his father. Lorenzo Card had called him last night and told him that Lewis had gotten some information. James wanted to talk with Lewis rather than simply get a name over the phone; he'd be able to ask a couple of follow-up questions in person. James thought it best not to bring Kenny along; he did not want to get him any further involved in case this whole mess went south.

Spring had sprung in Philadelphia; it was a seventy-degree, sunny day as he drove through West Philly for the 4:30 meeting. It looked like the whole family was waiting on the patio, including a German Shepherd that Lewis was restraining as James walked up their sidewalk.

"He'll calm down once he gets to know you, James," Lorenzo called to James. James came up the steps, and Lorenzo said, "This is my wife, Gladys. I don't think you met her last time." Gladys Card was about five-five, dark-skinned, and too stout for the jeans she wore. She gave them a pleasant smile as she offered her hand in greeting.

"I did not. Nice to meet you, Gladys. And the dog's name?" James said as it sniffed his leg and crotch. James held his breath hoping a quick sniff would satisfy the dog.

"Brewster, like after Punky Brewster," Lewis answered.

Brewster had settled down and sat next to James as he continued scratching the dog's ear.

Gladys said, "We thought it best to talk out here, out of the curious ears of our daughter."

"I appreciate that, and I don't think this will take very long, but I thought it best to see y'all in person than discuss over the phone. So, what did you learn, Lewis?"

"My friend don't want his name out there, and I assured him it'd be on the DL. He relaxed a bit. He said he got his weed from a kid they called Sneaky Pete. His real name is Peter Preston. He's a sophomore. I don't know him at all."

Leaning in and looking into Lewis's eyes, James asked, "Was that all?"

"I asked him if he knew where Pete got his stuff. He said that it used to be a guy by the name of JRo, but now it was a kid called News. His real name is Malcolm Newberry. I knew him a little bit. He graduated a year ago. He was known to be a druggie and not a ballplayer, so as I said, I didn't hang with the dude. He said that News mentioned once or twice a Mr. B, so I sensed that might be his contact."

"Can you tell me what this News looks like?"

"Better than that. Here's last year's yearbook." Lewis picked up the yearbook he had sitting next to him and opened the page he had marked with Newberry's picture. James took out his phone and zoomed in for a picture.

"This is great, Lewis. You are quite the sleuth. What are your plans after graduation?"

"Funny you should ask, Mr. McNeil. I'm interested in Criminal Justice, and Villanova and Temple both have good programs. I've been accepted to Temple and Wait-Listed at Nova. Temple would be much more affordable, of course."

"Sounds like a great plan. Congratulations Lewis."

Sensing the questions might be over, Gladys said, "I understand that Lewis's name will not be mentioned to anyone, neither students nor the police?"

"You have my word, Gladys. I cannot tell you how much I appreciate this. I think I mentioned the last time my theory is that Sherman Claxton learned or saw something he was not supposed to and may have been killed to keep that secret. If News is involved, it is more likely at the direction of Mr. B, but it's just as possible that neither is involved, and this will be a dead end."

Lorenzo added, "If Bo is innocent, we hope this helps, James. We'll be in touch should anything else come up. Good luck."

James thanked them again, patted farewell to Brewster, and left.

Chapter 58

April 26, 2022

Claudia was up early on a beautiful Saturday morning. She had invited her mom over for coffee this morning, and she was heading over to 4th Street Cookie Company in Manayunk for some sweet treats. They only carried cookies and brownies, but they were the best. She'd pick up a six-pack of assorted, and two brownies.

It was 8:50 when she got a call from her mom, who was waiting at the front door of the building, unable to enter. She told her she was a minute away, to come out, and she would pick her up.

They got into the apartment and Claudia put the treats out on the counter and asked her mom for coffee or tea; she opted for coffee, extra caffeine.

Winnie said, "Anything new with the trial? It's getting so close. I can't stand it." A tear appeared in the corner of her eye as she fidgeted with her coffee spoon.

"No, but I cannot imagine a jury would convict Bo with only that planted evidence. Not why I asked you here."

"OK!" Winnie looked up at her daughter, holding her breath.

"Mom, I think I'm a lesbian."

Her mom sat back; her eyes bulging. "You THINK? First Bo, now you. Is this contagious?"

"Get serious, Mom! You know Melanie, Bo's attorney? We had been out socially a couple of times, you know, just two girls having a drink and dinner. Last week after dinner, I invited her back here for dessert, and, well, I'll spare you the details. I'm going into town tonight. You know I had a couple of relationships with guys, but this was different. It was so real, so natural, so comfortable."

Winnie sat with a dumbstruck look on her face, resumed playing with her coffee, taking a sip, and said, "It's funny, Claudia, when Bo told us, I was not surprised at all, but I've gotta tell you, this does surprise me. With that said, I believe that God loves us all, and if He made you gay, then He loves gays. So, you have nothing to fear from us. I also believe in love, so why can't a woman love another woman, as well as a man? Do you have a plan?"

"What kind of a plan? This happened last week. I'm not certain if Melanie is still in the closet or what. I know that we really like each other and are going to continue seeing each other. We'll discuss all this as we go along. I'm not telling anyone yet, at least until I talk to Melanie and see where she is. If you feel you need or want to tell Dad, that's fine. I'll tell Bo eventually but might wait until his situation is resolved." Melanie had a smile and that glow of happiness that often accompanied a new romance.

"Claudia, I love that smile and glow you have. I hope only for your happiness. Thank you for telling me. Now, pass me a half of that brownie."

Winnie had told her dad, James, that she was having coffee this morning with Claudia. James decided to drive over to the Campbell house to confront Hugh about his poker game. He parked in front of the house, and Hugh was on the patio reading the *Daily News*.

"Winnie's over visiting with Claudia," Hugh yelled, trying to save James the walk up.

"That's good, Hugh, I'm here to talk to you."

"What'd I do this time, James?"

"You tell me!"

"Give me a hint!"

"How about poker at the 601?"

Hugh lowered his paper, now focused on his father-in-law, "Sheet! Whatta you know about that?"

"Not much, Hugh, just that you're losing money you don't have."

"Not true, James. Yeah, I've been losing a bit, but I've got it under control, and I'm only using the fun money I set aside for this purpose."

"Really? You're not into Bo's college money, are you?"

"Not that it's any of your business, but no, I have not touched that."

"Look Hugh, I know I can be a butt-insky, but we are all under a lot of stress and we will be until this Bo situation gets resolved. I don't want to have this discussion with Winnie, but I also don't want you gambling away your family's savings. I know that's a high-stakes game at the 601. Wasn't playing for quarters enough for you? How did you squirrel away enough to play at that level without Winnie knowing about it?"

"I'll play for another week or two. I think I have figured the game out. If I continue losing, I'll get out, OK?"

"I'll take your word on it, Hugh." *What was that expression, trust but verify?* James thought he needed to do both with Hugh, but he was OK for now.

"Phillies lost again last night; have they ever had a good April?"

"Not since 2008, but who's counting? You want some coffee?"

"Nah, I'm good. No need to mention my visit to Winnie."

Chapter 59

January 15th, 2022

The holidays came and went, mostly uneventful. Because Widener had a tournament over New Year's, Sherman was only home for three days at Christmas break. Bo and Sherman spent time at each other's homes, but their secret remained, so they were just "buddies." Jessica also had Christmas dinner with Bo's family since hers did not celebrate Christmas.

Jessica had started dating a young man from her neighborhood who had graduated from Lower Merion a year ago and was attending Penn. But she had plans to go to Northwestern University in September because of their outstanding journalism program and had no idea if or how any relationship with Glenn might survive those four years. Privately, she still hoped that Bo might switch teams back.

Overbrook and the other local high schools had a ten-day break, and Coach Rosen had only scheduled three practices. Overbrook was undefeated and, in five games, the closest had been a twelve-point win against Bartram. They played Lincoln Friday night and they expected that to be their toughest challenge to date.

Bo had signed a Letter of Intent to attend Villanova in September on a full Athletic Scholarship. Bo was relieved, and his family all seemed pleased with this decision. Under new NCAA rules, Bo could now be compensated for the use of his name, image, or likeness. The NIL rules and Villanova offered several agents that might represent Bo. The family asked James to look into this as he knew several agents from his entertainment business.

Now that Damian Mitchell and Donovan Washington knew about this News kid, they weren't sure what to do about him. This kid wasn't the brains of the outfit, of that they were certain. And if they confronted News and got the name of his boss, what then? Somehow, they didn't think, "Please, would you stop competing with us," would have much impact. If they were going to do anything, they would need to involve Heem.

Overbrook High had conducted the COVID-delayed locker search and had suspended three students for possession. Principal Phelps referred the students to Officer Armstrong, who said the Philadelphia District Attorney had no interest in prosecuting kids for minor drug possession, so why bother giving the kids a police record? So much for "Zero Tolerance."

Early in 2022, it seemed that everything and everyone was in its place; it was what it was.

Chapter 60

April 23, 2022

James McNeil reached Detective Vernon Brown on his cell phone at 7:30 in the morning.

"Hey James, what has you up at this hour? This business or pleasure?"

"Yes, good morning to you, Vern. I'm hoping I might borrow one of those zoom cameras you guys use when you are spying on the bad guys. You got one?"

"I might be able to lend you one. Who are you zooming in on?"

"Oh, doing some bird watching."

"Come over to my driveway and you can zoom in on the pigeon that shits on my car every night. Seriously, James, you're not thinking of doing anything stupid, are you?"

"You know me by now, Vern, I only do stupid. Just playing a hunch."

"This hunch ain't gonna blow back on me, is it?"

"Who knows where the blow may go, my friend."

"I'll drop it off on the way home, probably about six. Have the bourbon waiting."

"Seems reasonable. See you then, Vern."

At 5:50, Vern pulled up and parked in front of James's house; he could see James and his wife, Linda on the patio. They greeted and hugged, Linda asked about Vern's wife, Ronnie, and she excused herself to let the guys talk.

James had Vern's bourbon waiting, neat, as he knew he liked it.

Vern handed him the camera. "You know how to work this thing?"

James replied, "Let me see it. I used to have one at the studio, so I know a thing or two about them."

Taking a sip of his drink, he said, "You telling me your plan?"

"You really want to know Vern, or would you prefer to keep your deniability?"

"Tell me the plan, then I'll decide."

James continued inspecting the camera, getting comfortable with it. "We have discussed this before, and I think we agree that Sherman's murder in some way was drug-related. If not, why the cocaine in Bo's locker? Kenny has talked to Brahim Jones and has been assured that neither he nor his guys had anything to do with Sherman's murder. That leaves only this other drug gang; you recall that Jason Rogers murder, right? It's still unsolved. Rogers seems to have been replaced by a kid named News. Only other gang that seems to be active in the West Philly schools. Make sense so far?"

"Yes, if we believe Brahim, and of course, assume that Bo did not do it, placing his glass back down on the coffee table.

"We do, and he didn't. I've identified a couple of kids on this gang, but one is a sophomore at West Philly, and News graduated last year. Clearly, there has to be an adult supplying and directing these kids. For whatever reason, I want to believe this hit was his doing. All I know is they call him Mr. B. My plan is to tail this kid and see when he meets with Mr. B and get a picture."

"And then what?"

"I'm not certain, Vern. I have no intention of confronting him. I still do not have any evidence for sure, so I think I'd have two choices: tell Fred Chasnoff and have his investigator go after him, or tell you. Or, of course, I could tell you both. What would you do if I gave you this Mr. B?"

"I'm not certain, James. As you said, we still would not have any evidence, and I'd need to discuss it with my captain and the DA. The DA might have a problem with me trying to prove Bo's innocence. The trial is only a couple of weeks away. My first thought would be to arrest and put the squeeze on this News kid. See if he'll give up Mr. B. But he might not even know about Sherman's murder.

"Two requests, for now, James. First, please contact me if you learn or see anything. If you feel you need or want to also tell Chasnoff, that's fine. Secondly, please be careful. We don't want another Vladimir Petrov setting out to kill you."

"I'm all for avoiding that, Vern."

Chapter 61

April 24, 2022

Melanie Wexler had called for a pre-trial meeting and in attendance in their Bala office were Claudia, Bo, their investigator Tyrone Hill and, paralegal, Trudy Holler. Introductions and pleasantries were exchanged, drinks poured, and the meeting was called to order.

Melanie started, "We are two weeks from the trial, and I have not heard anything from the DA's office about dropping the case, so we must proceed on the basis we are going to trial. Ty, have you found anything at all that might help?"

"I wish I had better news, but I got nada. Whoever did this, they covered their tracks. No prints, witnesses, or leads. Bo, I know we have discussed this, but did Sherman ever let on that he knew or learned anything about the drug situation at West Philly? That has been our premise all along."

Bo frowned at Ty's lack of progress, but replied, "No! We met at The Palestra. Usual small talk before the game. Once the game started, we were in analysis mode, you know that play or player did this or that. We took the subway home after, but we got off at different stops."

"Our defense will begin with the cross-examination of their witnesses. First, no doubt, will be the coroner who will simply testify on the cause of death and that the forensics point to the murder weapon. We'll, of course, cross-examine and make her say that they did not find your prints or any evidence on the weapon or Claxton's body.

I suspect they will then call Deforia Weeks, who will testify he saw you two at the Reading Terminal Market, and you appeared to be romantically involved. The DA will be insinuating that the relationship may have been a motive. I'll get him to state that he knows nothing for certain about the relationship or any friction in the alleged relationship."

Bo had steepled his hands as if in prayer, and asked, "No way to avoid this, huh?"

"Not our call, Bo. Sorry. It's the only possible motive the DA has, and they must plant it. Then they may or may not call this Willie Heyward, who can only say he saw a tall Black man following Sherman the night of the murder. I'll get his testimony countered by having him admit that he cannot say with any certainty that this was you.

Next and lastly, Detective Brown will testify about the evidence they found in your locker. This is, of course, the most damning evidence. On cross, I'll tear into his ass about never verifying, having no fingerprints, that they never identified the informant, and that they never searched for any other suspects. Too neat and tidy."

"And our defense?" Claudia asked.

"That's why I started with our cross-exams because we do not have any witnesses or evidence that Bo was not at the crime scene. No one on the subway, bus, or bus driver, so we will call character witnesses, Bo's coach, perhaps the Principal or Officer Armstrong to confirm you have never had any disciplinary issues, etc. Bo, how would you feel about my calling Jessica Marks and Carl Watkins to confirm that you and Sherman had never had any disputes and, to the best of their knowledge, your relationship was solid?"

"I guess if I'm to be outed anyway, and this can help, I'd be OK, and I'm sure they will be."

Claudia asked, "Will you call Bo to testify?"

"I know on TV they always say the defendant should never testify, and while that is generally true, I'm not certain that would be the case here. I will seriously consider it and, of course, prep you, Bo. I would simply ask you to testify that you were in a relationship with Sherman, that you cared for each other deeply, and that you'd never harm him. And that you have no idea how the stuff got in your locker and that you've never touched any gun or bag of cocaine.

"The DA will have a tough time contradicting or tricking you into saying anything incriminating. I think you would be an effective witness.

Turning to the paralegal, Melanie asked, "Trudy, would you look into this? Find out about the locks on these kids' lockers, who has access to them, and how difficult they might be to open."

"I'm on it, Mel."

"Any questions or suggestions?"

Claudia spoke again, "I hate to ask you this, Melanie, but how are you feeling about this?"

"Natural question, Claudia. I cannot believe any jury could convict a seventeen-year-old of murder with such flimsy evidence. I'm still surprised they are going forward with the trial. I only regret not being able to offer another suspect, but perhaps Ty will still deliver on that."

"Let's not forget my grandfather. I know he's still chasing leads," Claudia added.

"If that's it, we are adjourned, and I'll be in touch with you all."

Chapter 62

February 9, 2022

Sherman Claxton had one of those rare in-season three-day weekends; no games scheduled, and the coach gave them off. He was heading home after his 3:00 English Lit class; rush hour on I-95 started earlier on Friday afternoons, and he probably would hit it. He knew an alternate route using Chester Pike through Delaware County and Southwest Philly, but it would probably take him just as long, and he'd have traffic lights every other block. He'd make that call when he got on I-95.

Tonight, he would catch up with a couple of his old West Philly teammates. Then tomorrow night, Villanova was leaving tickets for Bo for their game at The Palestra versus LaSalle. That would be a blast and some private time with Bo.

He had spoken with his mom last night and she asked him if he might stop by the 49th Food Market and pick up an order she would call in. She told him that she usually walked to the market but was ordering a two-liter bottle of Coke along with all the other stuff, and it might be too heavy for her to carry. He, of course, told her it would be no problem.

At 4:45, he pulled into the small parking lot at the Food Market and found a spot in the back. He went to the store's Pickup station and waited while the clerk finished with another customer. When she left, the middle-aged, matronly-looking clerk asked, "How may I help you?"

"I am here to pick up an order for Mrs. Claxton."

"Are you her son, Sherman?"

"Yes, ma'am!"

"Glad to meet you, Sherman. She talks about you all the time. I'll have Rodney bring the order right up." She called Rodney and reminded him there were two bags; one was in the refrigerator.

Five minutes later, Rodney arrived with the two bags in a shopping cart. "Can I help you to your car, sir?"

"Nah, if I can use the cart, I'm good, thanks. Is this paid for?"

Rodney checked the slip stapled to the bag and said, "Yep, all taken care of."

Sherman thanked him, waved to the clerk, and headed to his car. As he approached his car, he noticed two guys in the corner of the lot, standing behind a Ford Explorer with an open trunk. He recognized the younger one; it was News Newberry. He had been in a couple of his classes; he did not know him well, but he didn't want to appear rude, so he waved to him. When Newberry waved back, the other fellow glanced over. He was much older and could have been News's dad, but he looked familiar. They were both holding identical backpacks. Mysteriously, they both looked surprised; no, Sherman thought, shocked was a better word. They both turned their backs toward Sherman, *Don't worry, I've got no interest in talking to you*, Sherman thought to himself.

Sherman put the bags in the car and returned the cart. He got into his car, backed out of the spot, and glanced toward Newberry and his friend. They were peering over their shoulders as Sherman pulled away. *What the hell was that about, and who was that guy? Could he be a teacher? Talking to News in the Market parking lot? Not likely!*

"Holy shit!" Mr. B exclaimed. Realizing that Sherman had been staring at them, he yelled, "We are totally fucked!"

"What do you mean? How would he know you?"

"Oh, I don't know. Over the last three years, we played West Philly a dozen times, and he came to many other of Bo's games. He'd have to be a crackbrain not to recognize me."

"Nah, you're cool, Uncle Mac; he was too far away."

"Look, Mal, if he places me, I'm done. I could do two dimes in the slammer. I can't take that chance. Let me think on this; don't tell a soul. Do you know where Claxton lives?"

"It's in last year's school directory. I've got it at home."

"OK, I'll give you a call tonight on your burner phone. Keep it on vibrate. Get outta here now."

Malcolm Newberry started walking toward his home. He was scared shitless. *If Uncle Mac was in trouble, I'm in trouble*, he thought to himself. He knew that Uncle Mac would think of something.

Chapter 63

April 26, 2022

The last two days, James and Kenny had parked on Walnut Street with a clear view of the 49 Stop Food Market parking lot. Lewis Card's friend had told them that was where he met Sneaky Pete. The first day, they got pictures of Pete meeting with a girl; she appeared to be buying stuff. They got pictures to test the camera. The shots were good; both kids could be clearly identified. The next day, they saw nothing. They were wondering if this was the best way to catch a thief.

Today the lot was less than half full. This was not unusual as most of the customers were able to walk to it, many bringing a pull cart to carry their groceries home. The market was not that busy and no one was paying attention to two Black guys with a photo lens camera.

It was on the cool side, overcast, and off and on drizzling. James and Kenny both had caps and rain gear on. Kenny wore sunglasses too. They were nursing their third cup of coffee. They took turns using the market's men's room. They also took turns using the binoculars, hoping to spot this News kid.

James asked Kenny, "What's with the shades, Godfather?"

"If this goes bad, I don't want anyone to recognize me."

"I'm sure that'll fool them, Kenny."

At 4:40, Kenny said, "Hey James, I think that is News walking into the lot. The short thin kid in the red sweatshirt, with the black backpack." He passed the binoculars to James. But James preferred to use the zoom camera at this point. He focused on the kid and quickly confirmed that this kid was News.

They watched him walk casually toward the rear corner of the lot. A tall, older Black man got out of a Ford Explorer and went to the rear of the car, opening the hatch on the SUV. James focused on this guy as News got closer. "Holy Shit!" James exclaimed, "Holy Shit!"

"Whatta see, James?"

"Ignoring Kenny, James now had both faces in view as they exchanged backpacks. He took six snapshots and checked them to make certain they were clear. Their business concluded, News took off, and the older guy got back into his SUV. After the man backed out, James had a clear view of the license plate and took two more shots of that. The SUV pulled off.

"You gonna tell me what's going on?"

James sat there and again reviewed all the pictures he had taken. He looked at Kenny and, for the third time, exclaimed, "Holy Shit."

"It's clear that the shit is Holy, James but tell me more!"

"I know this guy."

James left a voicemail message for Vernon Brown. "Hey Vern, where are you? We need to meet right now. Call me!" He and Kenny decided to stay parked on Walnut Street for a few minutes, hoping they would hear back from Brown. They could stop by there if he were still at the station; it was only a mile away and on their way home.

Chapter 64

February 10, 2022

Bo texted Sherman, "Hey Sherm, you awake?"

It took a moment but Sherm responded, "Sort of, Bo, but I needed to get up anyway. What's up?"

"Not much, I'm heading out to Ardmore for lunch with Jessica, and I just thought we'd make a plan for the game tonight. Let's take the subway. Parking is a bitch around The Palestra, and I'm not dropping $20 to park."

"I agree. What time is the game?"

"7:00. I'm taking the G Bus to the subway and I'll try to catch the train at about 6:15 at 63rd Street. You get on at 52nd Street. I'll be in the second car. We'll meet at the Will Call window if we miss each other. Make sense?"

"Absolutely, but you couldn't get Nova to send a limo for you?"

"Yeah, right. Maybe next year. See you tonight."

"You got it. Say hi to Jessica for me."

To say that Mr. B had a restless night would be a gross understatement. No matter what Malcolm thought, Mr. B had to assume the worst, that Claxton could and would identify him. He must know that Malcolm was dealing, and thus, he was his supplier and boss.

Pops Williams told him many years ago that he had to be prepared to kill one day when he got into this business. It might be a competitor, a runner, a customer, or a supplier, but someday...

It seemed someday was today. Five years ago, he had bought an unregistered gun and silencer on the street and had practiced at Belmont Plateau. He took out the gun last night and checked it over; it looked fine.

But, when and where, and do I involve Malcolm? he thought to himself. He would need Malcolm to drive if he did it on the street. *And what if Sherman tells Bo Campbell?* He could not kill them both. He'd prefer to do it at night. The sooner, the better. He did not know when Claxton would return to school, and he'd rather do it on the streets he knew here in Philly than on a college campus he knew nothing about.

He formulated his plan and texted Malcolm, *if you're alone, call me.*

His phone rang within seconds. "Malcolm, I've got a plan. You probably won't like it, but I'll need you to drive my car. I'll pick you up at four. We'll follow Claxton tonight." He hung up, not giving News a chance to ask any questions or come up with an excuse. They would follow Claxton, and hopefully later, after dark, Claxton would be alone, and Mr. B would do it right on the street. He'd then jump into the car, and Malcolm would drive off.

If tonight didn't pan out, he would go day to day until the opportunity presented itself. And when Claxton was gone, he had a plan to frame Campbell: a lover's quarrel. Serve the fags right.

Chapter 65

April 26, 2022

"Papa James, everything all right?" Claudia answered her cell phone.

"Yeah, sure. You still at work?" James McNeil asked his granddaughter.

"Yep, what's going on?"

"Kenny and I may have solved the case. We have been tailing this drug kid, News, and we got pictures of him with Mr. B. You must get this to Chasnoff or Melanie right away." He continued to tell Claudia the details of their surveillance and pictures.

"Oh my God, this is unbelievable! Who else knows?"

"Only Kenny. I'm waiting to hear back from Vernon. A slight problem is that there is still no evidence for a murder charge. I'll call you again after I speak with Vern."

"This is great, Papa. Be careful. Let Vern do his job." Everyone knew of James's tendency to go too far.

As he hung up from Claudia, his cell phone rang; Vernon called back.

"Hey Vern, where are you?"

"Still at the station. What's up?"

"Hold on to your seat. I'll be there in ten minutes."

Eight minutes later, James McNeil and Kenny Anderson walked into the station at 55th and Pine Streets. Vernon was in the small lobby waiting for them.

"Sounds important. Let's go in here." Vernon led them into a small conference room just off the lobby.

They sat, and James set up his camera. "OK, you know we've been tailing this News kid, right, hoping he'd lead us to his boss, Mr. B?"

"Yeah?"

James proceeded to show Vernon the pictures slowly, one at a time. Vernon watched quietly without comment but with raised eyebrows.

"This is the mysterious Mr. B? He looks familiar. You know him?" he asked James.

"You don't, Vern? That's Reggie McIntosh, Big Mac, Overbrook's Assistant Coach."

"Holy shit! Are you sure? Of course, you're sure, or you wouldn't be here. So, this may prove or suggest that Big Mac is involved with drugs. Not knowing what's in the backpacks, it's not evidence, and still a huge leap to Sherman's murder. What's the motive?"

"As we've suspected all along, Sherman maybe saw exactly what we did, News and Mac exchanging backpacks, but maybe Mac saw Sherman and thought Sherman had recognized him. Mac was using this Mr. B alias, so he was paranoid about anyone discovering his identity. This News kid might not even know, but Sherman would have."

Vernon countered, "OK, if Sherman knew about Mac, why did he not tell Bo? That would have been his first call, I would think."

Kenny said, "Suppose Sherman didn't get a good look, or like Vernon, he couldn't place the face?"

"I knew I brought you along for some reason," James added. "Sherman did not know, or didn't know for sure, but Mac assumed he did. He couldn't risk it, thus, he needed to get rid of Sherman to protect himself."

Vernon said, "All plausible, but I'm not certain it will be enough for the DA to drop the charges against Bo. This only proves that News and Big Mac know each other and have the same taste in backpacks. And why and how did he frame Bo?"

James replied, "I think we have gone as far as we can. I believe it is time for you detectives to start detecting. I recall Bo saying once that Mac had some kind of problem with him. He wasn't sure if it was jealousy or what. Or maybe Mac thought if he handed you a suspect on a platter with hard evidence, it would avoid any further investigation, which it did."

"I'm thinking out loud here," Vernon started, "I'll update the DA's office, of course, but they will want evidence. Then my partner and I will pick up this News kid and shake him down. I'm not certain yet how much I'll tell him, but I will probably tell him a witness came in and told us he saw him murder Claxton. See if he gets scared enough to give up Mac."

Chapter 66

February 21, 2022

It was 4:15, and Mr. B and Malcolm Newberry sat in the car outside of Sherman Claxton's home on Osage Avenue. They knew Claxton was home as his car was parked in front of the house.

Mr. B had only told News about the tailing part of his plan as he was not certain his nephew could handle all the details. The kid would learn more later, for sure.

Whatever he knew or suspected he knew, News was totally freaked out. He hadn't slept much last night. He found himself peeing every hour. When he got up, he got out of the house so his mom couldn't ask any questions.

He was afraid to ask Mr. B for any plan details, but he feared the worst. There was only one way to make certain Claxton told no one about Mr. B, right? And Mr. B had two ski masks sitting on the console between them. And this wasn't Halloween.

They took turns walking to Park Pizza, two blocks away, to relieve themselves.

It was not until 6:05 that Claxton came out of his house. To Mr. B's surprise, Sherman did not get into his car but walked down Osage Avenue toward 52nd Street.

"Where the hell is he going on foot?" Mr. B asked out loud, not expecting an answer.

"Don't know, could be meeting someone close by, I guess," News replied.

They got out of the car and decided to follow him on foot, as a slow creeping car would stand out. When Claxton reached 52nd Street, he made a left, heading north. They followed at a safe distance as Claxton passed Walnut Street. As they neared Chestnut Street, Mr. B exclaimed, "Got it! I recall Bo mentioning last week that Villanova arranged tickets for him for tonight's game at The Palestra. Claxton is probably taking the subway and meeting him there. No sense in following him down there. I'll check to see what time the game starts, and then we can follow it to see when it ends. You hungry?"

"I can always eat, but we still have maybe three hours to kill."

"Yeah, why don't we pick up Chinese at China Wok, get the car, and return to my place? We can watch the Villanova game there, and when it ends, we'll go back, hoping Claxton comes home alone the same way he left."

"Works for me."

It was 7:15 when they got back to Mr. B's apartment with Wonton soup, egg rolls, and Moo Shu pork. He placed the food on the coffee table in front of the TV and went for plates, utensils, and two IPAs from the Conshohocken Brewing Company. The Villanova-LaSalle game had just started, so they settled in.

Bo and Sherman did not connect on the subway, but when Sherman arrived at 6:45 at the Will Call Window in front of the Palestra, Bo flashed the tickets with a big smile.

"Yo, bruh!" Claxton called; they hugged and looked at the tickets.

"Great seats, my man, two rows behind the Nova bench, with the players' families. We may need to watch our language. Whenever I see the Cats on TV, there are always a couple of priests close to the bench."

"I think I can restrain myself for a couple of hours. If not, I'll go out into the hall. I promise I won't embarrass you."

They entered The Palestra, and Bo told Sherm, "Got to take a loop around the concourse. I do it every time I come here out of respect for the game. Someday, I hope my name is up here somewhere."

The concourse of the Palestra was a veritable museum of basketball and the Big Five, including pictures of the famous coaches, Jack Ramsey, Chuck Daly, Rollie Massimino, Fran Dunphy; the players who visited, including Wilt Chamberlain, Guy Rogers, Julius Erving, Lionel Simmons, Jerry West, Oscar Rogers, Bill Bradley, and Calvin Murphy, to name a few. Each Big Five school had its own wall featuring its greatest teams and players. Sherman had been here before and seen it all, but he allowed Bo to give him the guided tour.

They found their seats, and the player introductions had started. When the game was ten minutes old, it was obvious that LaSalle was outclassed, and Bo and Sherm's interest waned.

Bo asked, "What did you do today, anything?"

"Yeah, did I tell you my dad decided to redo the den in the basement? So, I helped him get up the old carpeting and get rid of some of the furniture. He's gonna put flooring in, a daybed, TV, etc., and it should be nice. Oh, and yesterday something happened that freaked me out. I thought only old people forgot names and faces. I stopped by the market to pick up an order for my mom, and as I came back to the car, I saw this kid I knew from school. Malcolm Newberry. They call him News. He was a druggie, and I didn't know him well, really, just to see, I think he was in my algebra class.

"Anyway, in the parking lot, he's talking to an older guy whom I swear I know from somewhere, but I can't place it. I waved to News, but they both turned their backs to me when they saw me. It was totally weird."

"Hey, maybe he was buying drugs and didn't want anyone to see. I wouldn't worry about it."

"I'm not worrying about it. Just trying to place that guy's face. How about some popcorn, my treat?"

"I'm in, thanks, Sherm!"

At halftime, they went out to the crowded concourse and bought popcorn, a soft pretzel, and two Cokes. They looked around the crowd and spotted Jay Wright speaking with a woman. Coach Wright was dressed down for him, no three-piece suit, just a sports jacket and open-necked dress shirt. Bo said, "I should say hello, and thank Jay for the scholarship. C'mon." He tugged at Sherm's elbow.

"Excuse me, Coach Wright. Sorry to interrupt, but I thought I should say hello and thank you for any part you played in getting my scholarship."

"Bo Campbell." Wright smiled and extended his hand. "I'm glad you interrupted. Say hello to Lynn Tighe, our Associate Athletic Director. Lynn played at Villanova and has been here ever since. And I didn't help much in your recruitment Bo. Coach Neptune and his staff wanted you from the get-go."

Tighe extended her hand and said, "Very glad to meet you, Bo. We can't wait for you next season." Turning to Sherman, she said, "And you are?"

Sherman shook her hand and said, "I'm Sherman Claxton, a good friend of Bo's. Glad to meet you both."

Bo quickly added, "If his sweatshirt did not give it away, Sherman plays at Widener and had the weekend off. Thanks to whoever arranged the tickets."

"I can't take the credit for that either, but I'll pass it along to the coach," Wright responded.

There was a loud buzzer heard even out in the concourse; they all looked up and Tighe said, "The second half is starting soon. We better get back." They all shook hands again and returned to their respective seats.

"Wow, that's big time," Sherman exclaimed, clearly impressed, offering a fist bump and a big smile to Bo.

Forty-five minutes later, with Villanova leading by twenty-six points, they debated leaving, but Bo thought it might be in bad taste, so they stayed until the end.

Chapter 67

February 10, 2022

Since Bo and Sherman were getting off the subway at different stops, they decided to have a taco at the Taco Truck at 34th and Sansom Street on the way to the train. It had started flurrying, even though no accumulation of snow was predicted. It was too cold to stand outside and eat, and it was still early, only 9:30. They decided to go into the library and eat while pretending to read.

They grabbed magazines and tried to look like they belonged, even though it didn't seem as if the staff cared if they were a student or not.

"When you heading back to school?" Bo asked.

"My first class isn't until 11:00 on Monday, so either tomorrow night or perhaps Monday morning. You got games this week?"

"Yeah, Wednesday at Edison and then Saturday at noon, Bartram."

"You thinking you'll go undefeated?"

"I don't want to jinx us, but I think we are better than anyone we'll play. But you never know. That's why my grandpa always said, "That's why they play the games.""

Bo looked at his watch and said, "10:15. We gotta bounce. Hopefully, we can still catch a train at this hour; it's a long walk from here."

They returned the magazines, disposed of their trash, and resumed their trek to the 34th and Market Street subway stop.

Back on 52nd Street, Mr. B and News waited in the car. "Shit!" Mr. B exclaimed. "The game was over almost an hour ago. We may have missed them, or there was a change in plan, and Claxton stayed on the train with Bo. We'll give it until 11:00. If he is not here by then, we'll drive up to 63rd Street, where Bo would get off. If they are together, I'm not sure what I'll do."

"Is it time to tell me your plan now?" News asked.

"What do you think, Malcolm?" glaring at his nephew.

"I think you might do something I don't want to know about or be a part of."

"You're right. Just relax, will ya?"

Bo and Sherman got on the train at 10:30 and came out of the tunnel at 46th Street. It was still snowing. 52nd Street was the next stop.

"My stop, bruh. Talk to you tomorrow, and thanks again for the tickets."

"You got it, Sherm. Be careful."

They hugged, the train came to a stop, and Sherm departed with two other passengers.

At 10:40, their wait paid off; Mr. B spotted Claxton coming down the stairs from the subway platform. His Widener sweatshirt stood out, even though he had his hood up. Sherman walked south toward his home. Mr. B needed to give the details to Malcolm finally.

"Here's the plan, Mal. We'll follow him in the car along 52nd Street. Too many people here to do anything. I'll get out and follow him on foot when we get to Delancey Street. Osage is one-way, so you'll need to turn right on Pine, then left on 53rd. Wait at 53rd and Osage. That's where I plan to pop him and get in the car there. If there is anyone there, I'll have to abort and repeat this tomorrow. Any questions, Mal?"

"Isn't there any other way?" Malcolm yawned, a combination of weariness and fear.

"We have five minutes. If you've got one, now would be the time to tell me."

At the stop sign at Delancey, Mr. B got out of the car, holding the ski mask in his left hand and the gun under his jacket in the right. He was twenty-five yards behind Claxton; he'd stay at that distance until Claxton turned to Osage and gradually narrowed the gap.

Pedestrian traffic was lighter than Mr. B expected on 52nd Street; probably due to the snow. After they crossed Pine Street, he started closing in. A man was walking toward them; Mr. B turned his face toward the street, not wanting to be seen. As expected, Claxton turned right onto Osage. Mr. B was about fifteen yards behind him. When he got to 53rd Street, News was parked thirty feet from the corner, just far enough not to be noticed by Claxton.

When Mr. B reached five feet, Claxton had heard or sensed a presence. He turned and saw a man in a ski mask pointing a gun at him. Before he could scream, Mr. B fired two rounds into his chest. Sherman Claxton died before hitting the ground.

Mr. B turned, removed the mask, and quickly returned to the car. He got in and said, "Move out slowly, go straight down to Cedar, and turn right. Then pull over, and I'll drive."

Mr. B drove News home. "Lay low tomorrow. I'm going to school and will leave this gun and some H in Campbell's locker. I'll leave an anonymous tip so the police can find it. That should be enough for the police to arrest Bo and hopefully abort any investigation. We just need to resume our lives quietly. You, OK?"

Sniffling and near tears, Malcolm uttered, "Not really, Uncle Mac, but I'll deal with it. Talk to you next week."

Chapter 68

April 27, 2022

Detectives Vernon Brown and Roberta Rumson were sitting outside Malcolm's house on North Peach Street in an unmarked car and had been for the past hour. They had not seen anyone leave, so they assumed he was in the house. They hoped they might catch him outside to avoid involving any family members, but they decided they could not wait any longer.

Brown knocked on the door, and a woman opened the door. "Yes?"

"Mrs. Newberry? I'm Detective Brown and this is my partner, Detective Rumson. Is your son home?" They flashed their badges as they stepped into the small foyer.

"Yes, what's this about?"

"We need to ask him a few questions?"

"About what?"

"Would you please get him, Mrs. Newberry?"

She went up the stairs, presumably to question and retrieve her son. They could smell bacon either cooking or recently devoured in the kitchen. The home was neat but not extravagant. The family pictures seemed only to include three, Malcolm, his mom, and what appeared to be a sister. No man in the picture.

Mrs. Newberry came down the stairs with her son trailing.

Brown said, "We'd like to go down to the station and ask you a few questions, Malcolm."

"About what?" Malcolm asked.

"We'd rather discuss that at the station."

"Is he under arrest?" his mother asked.

Brown replied, "He is not, but we can get an arrest warrant if he refuses to come."

"Can I come with him?"

"You can, but you cannot be in the room when we are questioning him. It might be best that you wait here. We will get him back here; your call."

"I better go with you. Let me check the kitchen first, make sure nothing is cooking."

She returned, and they all left in Brown's car. They were quiet during the fifteen-minute ride to the station at 55th and Pine. They parked and entered the back door of the station. Rumson escorted Mrs. Newberry to the front lobby and asked the Day Sergeant to look after her. She then joined Brown and Malcolm in the interrogation room.

Vernon Brown began, "Malcolm, as we told you, you are not under arrest, but I want to record this session. I will read you your rights, and you may at any time request this interview be terminated, or you may ask for an attorney." Brown read Malcolm his rights and then continued.

"Let me tell you what we do know, Malcolm. First, we know you are selling drugs and using runners in West Philadelphia and Overbrook High Schools, and others as well. We also know you are being supplied and managed by someone known on the street as Mr. B. How am I doing so far, Malcolm?"

"No comment!" crossing his arms over his chest in a defiant manner.

"Now things get worse for you. We have a witness who placed you less than fifty yards from the dead body of Sherman Claxton on the night of February tenth. Our witness did not see you shoot Claxton, but it doesn't matter. Whether you shot him or are only an accomplice, this was premeditated murder and carries a life sentence, with no chance of parole."

Brown thought this would be enough; let the young man think about this. He had no such witness, of course, but what's a little white lie between friends.

The silence had its desired effect. Newberry went pale; he stared at the ceiling, praying for divine intervention. None was forthcoming; he stared back at Detective Brown.

"I ain't killed Sherman Claxton. That's all I'm saying."

"We don't think you killed Claxton, but you were there for sure. *(Well, maybe)* That's why we are here talking, and you are not in a cell yet. We have spoken with the District Attorney and are prepared to offer you a deal. If you give us what we need to nail this Mr. B for the murder, we are prepared to go easy on the murder charge. You'll need to do some time on the drug charge, perhaps three-to-five years. Give you a chance to think about how you want to live the rest of your life. What do you think?"

"I think I need to talk to my mom, and maybe an attorney."

Brown turned off the recorder and asked Rumson to retrieve Mrs. Newberry. When they returned, Brown asked, "Do you want to talk to your mom in private or would you want us to stay?"

"Mom, I'm sorry, but you'll hear some horrible shit. If I tell you with them in here, it will turn out to be a confession. What do you think?"

"Oh God, what have you done, Malcolm?" Gasping and covering her mouth.

"These guys have offered a deal if I confess and give up someone else. I think it's a good deal, but I'll have to spend some time in jail."

"Sweet Jesus! My baby, what have you gone and done? Jail, really?" She started to weep, shaking her head, unwilling or unable to accept what she was hearing. Turning to Brown, Mrs. Newberry asked, "Will we get this deal in writing?"

"Absolutely! After we hear his story, we'll have this all put into writing."

"Are you sure, Malcolm?" She continued sobbing, and Rumson offered her a couple of tissues.

Brown turned on the recorder and said, "We are resuming our interview with Malcolm Newberry. His mother, Wanda Newberry, has joined us. Malcolm was read his rights earlier and has chosen to continue without an attorney. Go ahead, Malcolm, tell your story, then Detective Rumson and I will ask any remaining questions."

"Mom, you know I was doing weed and some other stuff in high school. I am not an addict, but I like getting high. Maybe a shrink can help me understand why. What you don't know is that Uncle Mac is the boss man. He gets the stuff from somewhere, and I handle it with the kids in school."

His mom interrupted, "Oh, Jesus, Mary and Joseph! My brother got you into this? I'll kill the bastard."

Brown said quickly and tersely, "Please, Mrs. Newberry, let Malcolm continue. Before you do, please confirm that your Uncle Mac, aka Mr. B, is, in fact, Reggie McIntosh."

Malcolm did, "Yes, it is Reggie McIntosh. A guy by the name of Jason Rogers, or JRo, was working for Uncle Mac, but he got killed a year ago. Uncle Mac didn't do it, but he came to me because he needed someone he could trust to protect his secret. I thought I could use the extra money and make a career and good money. My life was for shit anyway.

Things had been going OK I guess until last Friday. Uncle Mac and I were settling up at the market on 49th Street, and Sherman Claxton spotted us in the parking lot."

"Excuse me, can you describe 'settling up', please?" Brown asked.

"We usually met on Friday afternoons, and I gave him any money I collected during the week, less my percent, and he replenished my stash. We simply exchanged backpacks, so no one saw any money or stuff."

"Thank you, continue. You said Claxton saw this exchange in the parking lot?"

"Yeah, and Uncle Mac freaked out. I wasn't even sure Sherman saw him, but Mac said he couldn't take that chance."

Rumson asked, "Just how would Sherman know Reggie McIntosh?"

"Uncle Mac is the assistant coach at Overbrook. He said West Philly played Overbrook twice a year for the four years. Sherman played at West, and after he graduated, he occasionally came to practice. He was best friends with Bo Campbell. Mac assumed that Sherman knew him and might out him."

"OK, go on, Malcolm. What did McIntosh decide to do?" Brown asked.

"He didn't tell me right away but said we needed to tail Sherman until we could get him alone. Saturday night, we followed him and saw he was getting on the subway, and Mac realized Sherman was going to The Palestra with Bo. He assumed Claxton'd return the same way. We got some dinner and chilled at his apartment. We watched the game on TV so we knew when it would end. We went and parked near the 52nd Street station and waited until Sherman came along. Then we followed him, and Uncle Mac got out of the car and shot him. That's the whole story." Malcolm took a deep breath as if the worst of this ordeal was over.

"How and why did he frame Bo Campbell?" Brown wanted to know.

"I don't know how he got into Bo's locker, but he said that framing Bo might terminate any investigation that might lead to us, and he said it 'would serve the fags right.' His words, not mine."

Mrs. Newberry just sat there crying and could not speak. Brown had seen many families destroyed by drugs, but he never stopped feeling sorry for the survivors. She no doubt would blame herself, an absentee father, and of course, her brother.

"We are not done. The DA wants more evidence against McIntosh. We'll need you to wear a wire to your next meeting this Friday. We'll coach you on what to say. You'll also need to testify in court. That will be part of our agreement." Turning to Rumson, Brown asked, "Roberta, would you get this statement and our agreement typed up, please?" Brown asked as he removed the tape and handed it to Rumson.

"This could take a half hour or so. Can I get you anything?" Rumson asked.

Malcolm replied, "Some water might be ok. Thanks."

Chapter 69

April 27, 2022

With only two days away, Vernon Brown had a lot to do before Friday's sting." But he wanted to do the fun stuff first, now that they had a signed confession and deal with Malcolm Newberry.

The first call was not to James McNeil *(surprise)* but to Michelle Pugh in the DA's office.

"Michelle, Vern Brown here. The deal is done, confession and the deal. How do I get the charges against Bo dropped?"

"I know how anxious you are to do that, but consider for a second if he or his family tell anyone or any of dozens of other possibilities, and McIntosh learns it, he could be in the wind. I'd prefer to wait until Friday after he's nailed."

"Suppose I try to talk to the family privately and get their assurance of confidentiality? No one is to know outside the five of them. You know I must call Chasnoff's office, and they're going to scream to have the charges dropped immediately."

"Shit, you're right, Vern! How about I call Melanie Wexler and tell her you are tracking down Bo and his parents? I'll tell her, and you tell them if ANYONE leaks Bo's innocence, they'll be arrested for interference. OK?"

"That works, Michelle, thanks. Tell her to please not call Bo or his family. That I'm heading out there now."

"Vern, I know you believed in Bo's innocence from Day One, and I started to hope you were right. Great job proving it."

"Thanks, but I had a lot of help, starting with Bo's grandfather. I'll call you soon."

Brown called James McNeil and said, "James, Vern. Can you gather Bo and his immediate family over at their house quickly? I'll meet you there."

Before James could ask what this was about, Brown hung up.

He checked in to see that Rumson was moving on the wiretap warrant, and he rushed out to his car. Fifteen minutes later, he pulled up in front of the Campbell residence but only Bo and his mom were on the patio. Just then, James pulled behind him. They walked up together.

Winnie Campbell said, "Claudia said she's two minutes away and Bo's attorney needs to be present."

Brown smiled, and they waited. But not for long. Claudia screeched to a halt, parked, and jumped out of the car.

"Where's Dad?" Claudia yelled as she joined the group.

Winnie answered, "Can't get here for an hour, he said to go ahead, and I'd call him with the update. Let's go inside; it's more private."

They all entered and stood in the living room with all eyes on Vernon Brown. These eyes were a mix of hope, fear, and prayer. They seemed to be holding their collective breaths and holding on to each other. Vernon had trouble keeping calm with a straight face. Then suddenly, he couldn't.

"Bo's off. He's innocent. The DA is dropping the charges."

There were screams of joy, smiles, and tears of joy. Vernon begged them to shush; there was more. Bo went over and threw his arms around Vernon Brown, "Thank you for giving me my life back. I don't know how to thank you."

James, of course, had to know, "What happened, Vern? Did you catch the doer?"

"We did, with your help, of course, James. And y'all know the murderer-Reggie McIntosh. But we have one problem. We need more evidence and have set up a sting on Friday to catch him on tape confessing."

"Before you go on, Vern," Claudia interrupted, "I know something you don't. Do you recall Chasnoff's paralegal, Trudy Holler? Melanie asked her to look into the student lockers, access, combinations, etc.

and she learned that all the student lockers were replaced five years ago, but the lockers in the fieldhouse were replaced with the same lockers two years ago. And there is one master combination for all the lockers. Thus, McIntosh would have access to all the lockers. No one in the Admin Office knew this."

Brown continued, "I'm sure I don't want to know how or when you learned this, but as I was saying about this sting, we have set it up on Friday. The DA fears that if word gets out that the charges against Bo have been dropped, McIntosh could take off, never to be seen again. Y'all must swear to me that none of this is made public to anyone outside this room, except for Hugh, of course, until you hear from me, hopefully, late Friday. Can I count on y'all to keep this secret? The DA has threatened arrest for anyone who leaks it."

The family looked at each other with smiles, they hugged each other and dried their tears. They were still all so happy they wanted to shout it out to the world, but James said, "We can do this. We have waited almost three months for this day, and we can wait two more days, right gang?"

"We can do this," Winnie assured Vernon, and they all nodded.

Vernon quickly added, "This includes Claxton's parents. I'll go tell them after the arrest."

James said, "Vernon, I need to thank you on behalf of our family. I never thought any good could come from my father's murder, but our friendship belies that. Thank you, my brother."

The family all smiled and cheered, "Amen!"

Vernon was too choked up to say anything, so he smiled, mumbled something about talking soon, and left. The Campbell family, relieved that their nightmare was now over, shared a group hug.

Chapter 70

April 29, 2022

It was 4:00 on an overcast but dry afternoon. Vernon Brown sat in the back of a white, unmarked van with two members of the department's surveillance team. They parked on 48th Street, a block away from the 49 Stop Food Market. They had been there for two hours, setting up and testing the equipment.

Roberta Rumson was on the ground inside the Market. The plan was that when Brown thought he had sufficient evidence on tape, he'd give her the green light to move in while he ran down to help in the arrest.

Malcolm Newberry had confirmed the 4:30 meet, and he was wired and prepped. Vernon could only hope the kid could go through with this. There was no turning back; if the confession did not happen today, they would regroup to find more evidence or set up another sting. They even considered bringing McIntosh in and playing the same story they had with Newberry and see if he would confess to save his nephew.

At 4:30, it was quiet in the van and Roberta confirmed that neither had appeared yet. They had contacted Malcolm who said his uncle was often late.

At 4:40, Roberta confirmed that McIntosh's Ford Explorer had pulled in and parked in the rear corner. She could see Malcolm walking toward his uncle. It was go-time!

McIntosh got out of the car as he saw his nephew approaching. He popped the trunk and greeted Malcolm. "What's going on, Mal? Did we have a good week?"

"Good and maybe bad too, Uncle Mac. Sales were good." He handed Mac his backpack. "But the cops arrested Sneaky Pete for possession with intent to distribute. He hasn't been released yet."

"Shit! How'd you find out about it?"

"Dwight Bridges saw it go down. Cops were staking out the parking lot at the CVS across from the school."

"OK, but Petey doesn't know that I exist, does he?"

"He knows that I exist, Uncle Mac. What if they offer him a deal to give me up? And Sneaky knows that Mr. B exists, but not your identity. If he gives me up, I could get a nickel in the joint. This ain't my first offense. It could get worse. Suppose they match the stuff they got from Petey to the stuff you left in Campbell's locker. They could charge me with murder."

"That's a huge leap, Mal, but I appreciate your concern. Trust me. I'll never let you take the hit for the murder. Should they ever charge you for that, I'll take off, and from wherever I wind up, I'll send them a confession, exonerating you. Got that?"

"Yeah, but maybe I should flee and stay with my Aunt Ethel down in Chester? If Petey gives me up, my mom will say that she has no idea where I went."

Vernon gave a small fist bump of success; he had heard enough. McIntosh had admitted to the murder, and with Newberry's collaborating testimony, they had McIntosh signed and sealed.

"Roberta, we're good. Move in slowly, I'm on my way. I doubt he's armed but be careful. Read him his rights and cuff him. I should be there by then."

"Gotcha Vern, I'm on the move."

Roberta Rumson left the Market and slowly walked toward McIntosh and Newberry. This was her biggest arrest ever and she didn't want to do anything that might jeopardize it now. When she got within ten feet, McIntosh looked up at her, just as she was removing her pistol.

"Reggie McIntosh, I am arresting you for the murder of Sherman Claxton. Turn around, and place your hands on the hood of the car. You have the right to remain silent ..."

"Not so fast, officer," McIntosh replied, grabbing his nephew around the neck and using him as a shield.

There goes my hope of an easy arrest, Rumson thought to herself. Her Plan B was to try to keep things calm while waiting for Brown or a negotiator to arrive.

Going unnoticed, a small crowd of shoppers had emerged from the Market and had clustered about twenty feet behind the officers. Cell phones were out, filming whatever was about to happen.

Vernon Brown and two police cars had appeared, and Vernon took over.

McIntosh turned around and looked at Malcolm. He tightened his grip on the kid and felt around for a weapon. "You set me the fuck up, Malcolm? How could you do this?"

"I'm sorry Uncle Mac. I didn't have a choice. They had me for the murder. I'm sorry!"

Unarmed and with six guns aimed at him, McIntosh knew he was delaying the inevitable. Brown had some training in hostage negotiation and knew job one was to keep the target calm, and talking. Brown turned to the officers and said, "Everyone remain calm and put your guns away. He appears to be unarmed and mine and Detective Rumson's guns should be enough to hold his attention."

Turning back to McIntosh, Brown said, "Reggie, I'm Detective Vernon Brown. We met once last year. I am a good friend of Bo Campbell's grandfather, James McNeil. You remember me? You don't really want to hurt your nephew, do you? He hasn't done you any harm."

Let him stew on this for a minute or two, Brown thought.

With all of the officers' eyes focused on McIntosh, one woman had taken a couple of steps forward from the crowd of on-lookers.

Dressed for grocery shopping in an Eagles T-shirt and jeans, wearing dark sunglasses, and carrying a 49 Stop Food Market plastic bag, she continued to slowly inch forward until she was next to the line of officers.

In one fell swoop, she reached into her bag, removed a gun, and darted toward McIntosh, shouting, "YOU KILLED MY BROTHER, YOU BASTARD!"

All eyes turned to her and McIntosh pushed his nephew away to defend himself, but it was too late. POW! POW! POW! She rapidly fired three shots into McIntosh's chest from four feet away. He fell to the sidewalk as blood pooled around him.

Brown and Rumson turned their guns toward her, but she had dropped her gun and fallen to her knees, sobbing hysterically. They approached her and Rumson retrieved the discarded gun. Brown kneeled and helped her to her feet. As they stood there, Brown saw her face for the first time. "I know you," he said, searching his muddled brain for how he knew this young woman. "You are Sherman Claxton's sister. Oh no! Why did you do this, Aaliyah? How did you know about McIntosh?"

It would be an hour later at the police station before she would be able to speak. Her parents had been summoned and arrived minutes later.

Brown looked one more time around the scene. Roberta had retrieved both backpacks, one with drugs, and the other with cash. He gave the thumbs-up sign, and they all left for 55th and Pine Street.

On the way, Vern made two quick calls: one to James McNeil, the other to the District Attorney, Michelle Pugh.

It was a good day, Vernon Brown thought to himself.

Epilogue

June 10, 2022

The Overbrook High School graduation started at 3:00 in the school auditorium. High School graduations predictably followed a traditional script; speeches about the bright futures the graduates could all look forward to, praise for the faculty, the parents, and the students who all contributed to the success honored this day. Then a valedictorian speech by one of the graduating class, special awards and scholarships, and at long last, the procession of graduates picking up their diplomas.

And this graduation would follow that script, with one unpredictable exception. When Bo Campbell was called to come forward to accept his diploma, the entire class, followed by all the other attendees, erupted into a standing ovation. The Principal, Clarence Phelps, realized he needed to allow this and held off continuing the roll call. He resumed when the applause had tapered off.

With the approval of the Campbell family, James McNeil and his wife, Linda, had planned a graduation party for Bo at the Hilton on City Avenue. Bo had approved so long as he could leave by 9:00 to join an After Party being held at Belmont Plateau in Fairmount Park for students only.

The graduation had ended at 5:30 and, by 6:00, the Bala Room at the Hilton was filled with Bo's friends and family.

James and his jazz group, the Sound Machine, provided soft music; the kids could get down with their rap and other loud music later. Vernon Brown and his wife Ronnie, and Roberta Rumson and her partner, Vanessa, were huddled around the quartet.

Jessica Marks did not bring her boyfriend and was clinging to Bo who was making the rounds, accepting congratulations, with many asking about Reggie McIntosh. Bo wasn't anxious to discuss and for the most part, just shrugged.

Claudia was arm and arm with Melanie Wexler, introducing her to friends and family. Few could tell if these were two friends or lovers, and Claudia made no effort to clarify. But she was glowing, as her mother had told her.

Bo and Jessica saw Mr. and Mrs. Claxton, Sherman's mom and dad, and headed toward them. As he neared them, they stepped toward him with their arms open, "Oh Bo, we are so proud of you, congratulations," Mrs. Claxton said.

Bo was near tears when he replied, "Thanks for being here, I wish so much that Sherman was here with us tonight. And how's Aaliyah?"

Mrs. Claxton replied, "We do believe that Sherman's spirit is here with us tonight, Bo. We must believe that. Aaliyah will be fine, we pray. It was my fault; when you called me in confidence to tell me they were arresting McIntosh for Sherman's murder, I was just so glad that I shared it with her. I never considered that she would do anything like this.

"We have an attorney and as yet, the DA has not brought charges."

Bo hugged the Claxtons again and spotted Jay Wright and Coach Neptune in conversation with his father. Bo dragged Jessica over toward them. "Mr. Wright, Coach Neptune, this is my friend Jessica. Thanks for being here."

"Hi Jessica, good to meet you. Thanks for inviting us Bo, and congratulations," Wright said, shaking Bo's hand and patting him on the shoulder.

"It's official now, huh, you're a Wildcat," Coach Neptune added, also exchanging handshakes.

"I'm excited. It's been a crazy year, but I stayed in shape and will play enough this summer to be sharp in the fall. I can't wait."

"Don't overdo it, Bo, and call me over the summer. We'll have you out and give you a one-on-one tour of the facilities."

"Thanks, will do. I'm taking off so thanks again for being here."

At 8:30, Bo walked Jessica out to the valet station. She had driven alone and said she did not wish to join him in Fairmount Park. She asked Bo, "What are your plans for the summer?"

"Nothing special. I intend to play in the Narberth League again but as you heard, the coach doesn't want me to overdo it. How come you didn't bring Glenn tonight?"

"He would not have known anyone, and I didn't know if this would be the last time I see you, so I wanted some private time."

As the valet drove up in Jessica's car, Jessica said, "One last question Bo, with Sherman gone, you think there is any chance you might switch teams again?"

Embracing her and realizing the significance of her question, he replied, "Maybe I will, Jessica. Maybe I will."

FRANK LAZARUS

THE END

AUTHOR NOTES

This story has been set in Philadelphia, my hometown, and its surrounding areas.

Kevin Bacon, who also grew up in Philadelphia, has been credited with coining the phrase, "It's a Philly Thing!" In their march to the 2023 Super Bowl, the Philadelphia Eagles and their fans embraced the phrase. When Bacon was asked about its origination, he said, "I got tired of trying to explain cheesesteaks, roast pork, and the Mummers to people, so I started to say, 'It's a Philly Thing.'"

Here is a partial list of some Philly Things:

Jawn

Yo

Scrapple

Roast Pork Sandwich

Cheesesteaks

Hoagies

Soft Pretzels

Jimmies

Pats/Genos/Jim's/D'Alessandro's

Art Museum Steps

Reading Terminal Market

Boathouse Row

William Penn

Vince Papale

Throwing Snowballs at Santa

Fishtown

Bernie Parent

Butterscotch Krimpets

Philly Special

Bassetts Ice Cream

The Philly Phanatic

Irish Potatoes
Wilt Chamberlain
The Big Five
Wiz
PSFS
Rocky
Bandstand
Hyskimarromcfadiozoo

If you do not know what any of these are, please don't ask. "It's a Philly Thing."

Many years ago, I thought I had one novel to write. This was that novel. Every five years or so, I would write another paragraph. This novel was going nowhere, very slowly.

Early in 2023, after retiring from the life insurance industry, the inspiration for *THE MURDER GAMBIT* came to me. If you have not read it yet, there is a life insurance connotation. There was no single protagonist in *TMG*, but Detective Vernon Brown and James McNeil, the son of one of the murder victims, emerged as key figures.

When completed, I wondered if Brown and McNeil might get a sequel. I dusted off the old novel, converted WordPerfect to Word, totally re-wrote the story, and *The Phenom* was born. And mentioning "rewrites", toward the end of my first draft, I realized I had totally forgotten about COVID, and much of the story took place in 2020. Rewrite, or ignore COVID? I chose to rewrite, but please forgive the liberties I took in resuming school, zoom classes, and kids out playing basketball. I did not want COVID to interfere too much with the story.

This book would not exist if it were not for the diligence and patience of my editor, Mary Walsh. Mary, you have my sincerest gratitude.

Mary is an accomplished author of her own, and I encourage you to visit: marywalshwrites.com[2]

I hope you enjoyed this story. If you did, I would appreciate your leaving a review on social media, Goodreads, or wherever you purchased the book. Reviews really help, and are sincerely appreciated.

And feel free to write to me at FrankLazScribe@gmail.com. I promise to respond!

Thank you for buying my book.

Frank Lazarus

---

2.   https://www.google.com/url?q=https://www.google.com/ url?q%3Dhttp://marywalshwrites.com/%26amp;sa%3DD%26amp;source%3Deditors%26amp;ust%3D1683036017304822%26amp;usg%3DAOvVaw0-3NxM8itFq-oUFb3X6mYt&sa=D&source=docs&ust=1683036017501546&usg=AOvVaw1k2xdowMpP1 6km_-H-xSox

PRAISE FOR THE MURDER GAMBIT

Timothy C. Flanagan

5 out of 5 stars

Great mystery story. Combination of John Grisham and Lisa Scottoline

Fascinating finish. Worth reading.

Jess Forden

5.0 out of 5 stars

Original story, great read

I've never read a murder mystery book with such a creative, original plot. The character reference page in the front was very useful! Loved the humor and frequent Philly name-drops.

Missi Gregory[1]

May 14, 2023[2]

What a great book by a new author! If you are a Philly native, I highly recommend it as it's loaded with all things Philly!

Jim J

Hi Frank! I just finished your book and absolutely loved it!!! Not usually the type of story that I would go for (usually like biographies or sports stories), but loved these stories as they developed, especially with Philadelphia as the setting, and found myself reading 25-30 pages at a time. What a talent you are! Thanks so much for signing my copy; now, I'll share it with my family. Hope you'll put pen to paper again, even though I'm sure it's a huge undertaking!

On Sat, June 17, 2023 at 5:30PM Charles S wrote:

---

1. https://www.goodreads.com/user/show/90905920-missi-gregory

2. https://www.goodreads.com/review/show/5540130863

Hi Frank! The grandkids are here, so I couldn't devote full time to reading your book. However, once I started it, it was hard to put down. I really enjoyed it and am looking forward to the next one. Good work. Charlie

AUTHOR'S PROFILE

Frank Lazarus was born and raised in West Philadelphia and attended Overbrook High School, as you may have guessed from his writings.

After graduating high school, Frank spent two years in the U.S. Army during the Viet Nam War. After his service, he completed his Bachelor's Degree in Business Administration at St. Joseph's University, in Philadelphia.

He was in the Financial Services and Life Insurance industry for fifty-three years before he retired at the end of 2021.

Frank has three adult children and five grandchildren.

Frank and his partner Deb spend their time on Hilton Head Island and Philadelphia.

Don't miss out!

Visit the website below and you can sign up to receive emails whenever Frank Lazarus publishes a new book. There's no charge and no obligation.

https://books2read.com/r/B-A-OKJAB-XEWNC

Connecting independent readers to independent writers.